Gemma and the
Ultimate Standoff

Gemma and the Ultimate Standoff

Shana Muldoon Zappa and Ahmet Zappa
with Zelda Rose

Disney Press

Los Angeles • New York

Printed in the United States of America
Reinforced Binding
First Paperback Edition, August 2016
1 3 5 7 9 10 8 6 4 2

FAC-025438-16169

Library of Congress Control Number: 2016930866
ISBN 978-1-4847-1431-7

SUSTAINABLE
FORESTRY
INITIATIVE

Certified Chain of Custody
Promoting Sustainable Forestry

www.sfiprogram.org
SFI-01054

The SFI label applies to the text stock

For more Disney Press fun, visit www.disneybooks.com

Halo Violetta Zappa. You are pure light, joy, and inspiration. We love you soooooo much.

May the Star Darlings continue to shine brightly upon you. May every step upon your path be blessed with positivity and the understanding that you have the power within you to manifest the most fulfilling life you can possibly dream of and more. May you always remember that being different and true to yourself makes your inner star shine brighter. And never ever stop making wishes.

Glow for it. . . .
Mommy and Daddy

And to everyone else here on "Wishworld":

May you realize that no matter where you are in life, no matter what you look like or where you were born, you, too, have the power within you to create the life of your dreams. Through celebrating your own uniqueness, thinking positively, and taking action, you can make your wishes come true. May you understand that you are never alone. There is always someone near who will understand you if you look hard enough. The Star Darlings are here to remind you that there is an unstoppable energy to staying positive, wishing, and believing in yourself. That inner star shines within you.

Smile. The Star Darlings have your back. We know how startastic you truly are.

Glow for it. . . .
Your friends,
Shana and Ahmet

Student Reports

NAME: Clover
BRIGHT DAY: January 5
FAVORITE COLOR: Purple
INTERESTS: Music, painting, studying
WISH: To be the best songwriter and DJ on Starland
WHY CHOSEN: Clover has great self-discipline, patience, and willpower. She is creative, responsible, dependable, and extremely loyal.
WATCH OUT FOR: Clover can be hard to read and she is reserved with those she doesn't know. She's afraid to take risks and can be a wisecracker at times.
SCHOOL YEAR: Second
POWER CRYSTAL: Panthera
WISH PENDANT: Barrette

* · · *· · ✦ · ·* · · *

NAME: Adora
BRIGHT DAY: February 14
FAVORITE COLOR: Sky blue
INTERESTS: Science, thinking about the future and how she can make it better
WISH: To be the top fashion designer on Starland
WHY CHOSEN: Adora is clever and popular and cares about the world around her. She's a deep thinker.
WATCH OUT FOR: Adora can have her head in the clouds and be thinking about other things.
SCHOOL YEAR: Third
POWER CRYSTAL: Azurica
WISH PENDANT: Watch

NAME: Piper
BRIGHT DAY: March 4
FAVORITE COLOR: Seafoam green
INTERESTS: Composing poetry and writing in her dream journal
WISH: To become the best version of herself she can possibly be and to share that by writing books
WHY CHOSEN: Piper is giving, kind, and sensitive. She is very intuitive and aware.
WATCH OUT FOR: Piper can be dreamy, absentminded, and wishy-washy. She can also be moody and easily swayed by the opinions of others.
SCHOOL YEAR: Second
POWER CRYSTAL: Dreamalite
WISH PENDANT: Bracelets

Starling Academy

NAME: Astra
BRIGHT DAY: April 9
FAVORITE COLOR: Red
INTERESTS: Individual sports
WISH: To be the best athlete on Starland—to win!
WHY CHOSEN: Astra is energetic, brave, clever, and confident. She has boundless energy and is always direct and to the point.
WATCH OUT FOR: Astra is sometimes cocky, self-centered, condescending, and brash.
SCHOOL YEAR: Second
POWER CRYSTAL: Quarrelite
WISH PENDANT: Wristbands

NAME: Tessa
BRIGHT DAY: May 18
FAVORITE COLOR: Emerald green
INTERESTS: Food, flowers, love
WISH: To be successful enough that she can enjoy a life of luxury
WHY CHOSEN: Tessa is warm, charming, affectionate, trustworthy, and dependable. She has incredible drive and commitment.
WATCH OUT FOR: Tessa does not like to be rushed. She can be quite stubborn and often says no. She does not deal well with change and is prone to exaggeration. She can be easily sidetracked.
SCHOOL YEAR: Third
POWER CRYSTAL: Gossamer
WISH PENDANT: Brooch

NAME: Gemma
BRIGHT DAY: June 2
FAVORITE COLOR: Orange
INTERESTS: Sharing her thoughts about almost anything
WISH: To be valued for her opinions on everything
WHY CHOSEN: Gemma is friendly, easygoing, funny, extroverted, and social. She knows a little bit about everything.
WATCH OUT FOR: Gemma talks—a lot—and can be a little too honest sometimes and offend others. She can have a short attention span and can be superficial.
SCHOOL YEAR: First
POWER CRYSTAL: Scatterite
WISH PENDANT: Earrings

Student Reports

NAME: Cassie
BRIGHT DAY: July 6
FAVORITE COLOR: White
INTERESTS: Reading, crafting
WISH: To be more independent and confident and less fearful
WHY CHOSEN: Cassie is extremely imaginative and artistic. She is a voracious reader and is loyal, caring, and a good friend. She is very intuitive.
WATCH OUT FOR: Cassie can be distrustful, jealous, moody, and brooding.
SCHOOL YEAR: First
POWER CRYSTAL: Lunalite
WISH PENDANT: Glasses

NAME: Leona
BRIGHT DAY: August 16
FAVORITE COLOR: Gold
INTERESTS: Acting, performing, dressing up
WISH: To be the most famous pop star on Starland
WHY CHOSEN: Leona is confident, hardworking, generous, open-minded, optimistic, caring, and a strong leader.
WATCH OUT FOR: Leona can be vain, opinionated, selfish, bossy, dramatic, and stubborn and is prone to losing her temper.
SCHOOL YEAR: Third
POWER CRYSTAL: Glisten paw
WISH PENDANT: Cuff

NAME: Vega
BRIGHT DAY: September 1
FAVORITE COLOR: Blue
INTERESTS: Exercising, analyzing, cleaning, solving puzzles
WISH: To be the top student at Starling Academy
WHY CHOSEN: Vega is reliable, observant, organized, and very focused.
WATCH OUT FOR: Vega can be opinionated about everything, and she can be fussy, uptight, critical, arrogant, and easily embarrassed.
SCHOOL YEAR: Second
POWER CRYSTAL: Queezle
WISH PENDANT: Belt

Starling Academy

NAME: Libby
BRIGHT DAY: October 12
FAVORITE COLOR: Pink
INTERESTS: Helping others, interior design, art, dancing
WISH: To give everyone what they need—both on Starland and through wish granting on Wishworld
WHY CHOSEN: Libby is generous, articulate, gracious, diplomatic, and kind.
WATCH OUT FOR: Libby can be indecisive and may try too hard to please everyone.
SCHOOL YEAR: First
POWER CRYSTAL: Charmelite
WISH PENDANT: Necklace

* · · * · · * · · * · · * · · *

NAME: Scarlet
BRIGHT DAY: November 3
FAVORITE COLOR: Black
INTERESTS: Crystal climbing (and other extreme sports), magic, thrill seeking
WISH: To live on Wishworld
WHY CHOSEN: Scarlet is confident, intense, passionate, magnetic, curious, and very brave.
WATCH OUT FOR: Scarlet is a loner and can alienate others by being secretive, arrogant, stubborn, and jealous.
SCHOOL YEAR: Third
POWER CRYSTAL: Ravenstone
WISH PENDANT: Boots

* · · * · · * · · * · · * · · *

NAME: Sage
BRIGHT DAY: December 1
FAVORITE COLOR: Lavender
INTERESTS: Travel, adventure, telling stories, nature, and philosophy
WISH: To become the best Wish-Granter Starland has ever seen
WHY CHOSEN: Sage is honest, adventurous, curious, optimistic, friendly, and relaxed.
WATCH OUT FOR: Sage has a quick temper! She can also be restless, irresponsible, and too trusting of others' opinions. She may jump to conclusions.
SCHOOL YEAR: First
POWER CRYSTAL: Lavenderite
WISH PENDANT: Necklace

Introduction

You take a deep breath, about to blow out the candles on your birthday cake. Clutching a coin in your fist, you get ready to toss it into the dancing waters of a fountain. You stare at your little brother as you each hold an end of a dried wishbone, about to pull. But what do you do first?

You make a wish, of course!

Ever wonder what happens right after you make that wish? *Not much*, you may be thinking.

Well, you'd be wrong.

Because something quite unexpected happens next. Each and every wish that is made becomes a glowing Wish Orb, invisible to the human eye. This undetectable orb zips through the air and into the heavens, on a one-way trip to the brightest star in the sky—a magnificent place called Starland. Starland is inhabited by Starlings, who look a lot like you and me, except they have a sparkly glow to their skin, and glittery hair in unique colors. And they have one more thing: magical powers. The Starlings use these powers to make good wishes come true, for when good wishes are granted, the result is positive energy. And the Starlings of Starland need this energy to keep their world running.

In case you are wondering, there are three kinds of Wish Orbs:

1) GOOD WISH ORBS. These wishes are positive and helpful and come from the heart. They are pretty and sparkly and are nurtured in climate-controlled Wish-Houses. They bloom into fantastical glowing orbs. When the time is right, they are presented to the appropriate Starling for wish fulfillment.

2) BAD WISH ORBS. These are for selfish, mean-spirited, or negative things. They don't sparkle

at all. They are immediately transported to a special containment center, as they are very dangerous and must not be granted.

3) IMPOSSIBLE WISH ORBS. These wishes are for things, like world peace and disease cures, that simply can't be granted by Starlings. These sparkle with an almost impossibly bright light and are taken to a special area of the Wish-House with tinted windows to contain the glare they produce. The hope is that one day they can be turned into good wishes the Starlings can help grant.

Starlings take their wish granting very seriously. There is a special school called Starling Academy that accepts only the best and brightest young Starling girls. They study hard for four years, and when they graduate, they are ready to start traveling to Wishworld to help grant wishes. For as long as anyone can remember, only graduates of wish-granting schools have ever been allowed to travel to Wishworld. But things have changed in a very big way.

Read on for the rest of the story. . . .

Prologue

"Quiet, please, everyone!" Gemma shouted.

She was immediately gratified when the room fell silent and eleven pairs of eyes--in varying shades of violet, rose, auburn, gold, green, and blue--looked up at her. Gemma wanted to make sure that all of the Star Darlings, who were sitting on the floor of Tessa and Adora's dorm room, were listening carefully.

Leona tossed her golden curls and grinned at Gemma, "That's rich, coming from you," she said. But her smile was warm and kind and Gemma grinned back at her. *It's funny, those could have been fighting words not so long ago,* Gemma thought. But the Star Darlings had been through so much since the school year began and they had learned so much about each other's personalities— their strengths, quirks, and foibles. Gemma now understood that Leona was just attempting to lighten the mood, not trying to provoke her. She smiled as she took in Leona and Scarlet, roommates who had once been at each other's throats (even before receiving the floral arrangements of negativity) now sitting side by side, almost leaning against each other. They still both possessed strong personalities, that was for sure, but they were learning to work together instead of against each other. And maybe even becoming friends in the process.

"Does everyone have a snack?" Gemma's older sister, Tessa, asked in a motherly tone. She was circling the room with a tray of pastries. Gemma knew that her sister had stayed up late the night before, making certain to prepare each Star Darling's favorite baked treat in her micro-zap.

"I'll take a moonberry tart!" called Cassie, her eyes glinting behind her star-shaped glasses.

"It's all yours," said Tessa enthusiastically. She took a step forward.

"*Starf!*" screeched Clover. "You're squashing my hand!"

"Oops, star apologies," said Tessa. Without thinking, she let go of the tray of delicacies and sent it floating toward Cassie.

"Hey, stop that!" said Adora. "You know we need to conserve all the wish energy we can!"

Startled, Tessa dropped the tray, which landed with a clunk on Cassie's head. "Ouch!" the tiny girl said, rubbing her head. Then she gave a cry of delight as she grabbed a pastry, oozing with moonberries, before it slid off the tray. She took a big bite. Her glowfur, Itty, once a secret but now known to all the Star Darlings, zoomed over for a cuddle and a bite of the treat. Itty's "Song of Contentment" filled the air and visibly relaxed everyone.

"Go ahead, Gemma," said Sage.

Gemma pulled up a holo-letter. It was a group effort, composed by all the Star Darlings after much discussion. Now they were ready to hear it read back to them. They would make any last-minute changes they deemed necessary and then send it out to its intended recipient.

"'Dear Lady Stella,'" Gemma read. "'We are writing to you because we have come to the terrible realization that we have made a mistake. . . .'"

Cassie raised an arm clad in a sheer silvery sleeve. "Can we get rid of 'terrible' and add 'unfortunate'?" she suggested. "I think it sounds a lot less judgy." Cassie's voice was clear but her eyes were downcast. Gemma knew that Cassie was feeling very guilty about spearheading the suspicion against their former headmistress.

Gemma looked over at Sage, who nodded. She started again: "'We are writing to you because we have come to the unfortunate realization that we have made a mistake. . . .'"

Vega raised her hand. "Yes, Vega?" Gemma said patiently.

"I don't think that's right," Vega said, her brow furrowed. "It's actually quite fortunate that we came to the realization that we made a mistake. Fortunate for all of us, including Lady Stella, actually. If we're going to change it, I think we should just say 'the realization.' Simple and effective."

Libby spoke up. "Why don't we call it a shocking realization? I mean, it certainly surprised all of us when we realized that Lady Stella was working with Sage's mom and that we were totally wrong about her."

"No, no, no," said Cassie, shaking her head emphatically. "I meant that we should get rid of 'terrible' and add 'unfortunate' before 'mistake.' The *mistake* was what was unfortunate, you see."

The girls started to chatter among themselves. Gemma made a face. They were never going to get the letter out to Lady Stella if they were going to deliberate over every word.

Then Astra stood up and gave a piercing whistle. That got everyone's attention. Itty's song came to an abrupt halt. Astra pointed to Gemma. "Let's just let Gemma read it through. We can comment when she's done. Go on, Gemma," she said.

Gemma cleared her throat and started over. " 'Dear Lady Stella, we have come to the realization that we have made an unfortunate mistake.' "

Gemma looked up. Cassie nodded, and everyone else seemed okay with the change, so she went on:

" 'We now know that you have been working with the noted wish energy scientist Indirra to come up with a solution to the wish energy crisis and are not causing it. We think we can help figure out who is the culprit: the same Starling who sent us the poisonous flowers that caused us to argue and provided us with the nail polish that made us act odd, and who has been controlling our missions and ruining our Wish Pendants . . .' "

Gemma made a point of not looking directly at Leona, who was actually the only Star Darling whose Wish Pendant had been ruined. She continued.

" 'There is one Wish Mission left to come. We have been hearing reports from our families and friends that the shortage is worse than we realized. We are worried that this is our last chance to collect enough wish energy to help reverse the crisis.' "

Gemma's glow flared orange. It was *her* Wish Mission and she was both thrilled and terrified at the prospect. Talk about pressure!

" 'Lady Cordial is trying her best, but it is clear that she is just not up to the job and may even be in denial about the severity of the shortage. We need your help and guidance. Won't you please come back and be our leader once more? Starfully yours, the Star Darlings: Sage, Libby, Leona, Vega, Scarlet, Cassie, Piper, Astra, Tessa, Adora, Clover, and Gemma.' "

She stopped reading and looked up. The group stared back at her silently and the mood suddenly felt tense to Gemma. Itty must have sensed it, too, because she gave a throaty purr and began to sing her "Song of Relaxation." Despite her anxiety, Gemma found herself calming down a bit as the comforting tune filled the air.

"I think it's ready to go," Sage finally said. "Is everyone in agreement?"

All the girls nodded and Gemma pressed the send button. As everyone stared at her expectantly, she felt like a few words were in order. But Gemma's mind began to race. Lady Stella was missing. It was their fault. There was a terrible energy shortage and only one mission—hers—left. She opened her mouth to say something reassuring, but nothing came out.

Well, that was a first.

CHAPTER
1

Gemma narrowed her eyes and scrunched up her face at her Star-Zap's screen, trying to use the sheer force of her will to make it chime and flash with an incoming message from Lady Stella. When she looked up, the rest of the Star Darlings were looking back at her oddly. *Must be nerves*, she thought. Everyone was on edge, waiting for the headmistress's response.

"Any starmin now," Gemma said encouragingly, at last able to speak. Her words came back to her in a rush. "Any starmin now I'm sure we'll be hearing from Lady Stella. Actually, she's probably holo-typing like mad right now, writing to let us know that there are no hard feelings! She's not one to hold a grudge. She's got to understand that all the evidence was clearly pointing to her. We actually had no choice but to believe she was the culprit." She caught her breath and thought for a moment, seeing the other side of the story. "Although, come to think of it, she actually could be quite angry. We *did* falsely accuse her of sabotaging us. And at the very least, she's most likely disappointed in us for not trusting her. I mean, she was our headmistress. What were we thinking!" Then, noticing the other Star Darlings' frowns, she did an about-face. "But . . . it's quite likely she will be simply relieved that we came around to believing in her. I mean, she just disappeared in a puff of smoke as soon as we started talking to her. What were we supposed to think? She could have explained everything, convinced us we were wrong. Instead, she vanished! Well, hopefully she's forgiven us and she'll have an idea about how we're supposed to save Starland that she'll share with us. We certainly haven't been able to figure that out on our own! Oh, my stars, I just hope she's not mad at us for doubting her. The truth of the matter is that we really should have—"

"Gemma!" said Adora in a warning tone.

"Yes?" said Gemma, turning toward the tall, slender girl with the sky-blue aura. Gemma had just been getting warmed up and, frankly, resented the interruption. So she had raised some uncomfortable points. They were all true, weren't they?

Adora's response was to put both index fingers to her temples in the classic Starlandian "zip it" signal. Gemma gave the girl a "What in the stars do you mean?" look. Gemma couldn't stand uncomfortable silences, and it looked like the rest of the girls were feeling the same way. Like Piper, for example. Although she had just begun to meditate, her long seafoam-green ponytail draped over her shoulder like a lovely ripple of seawater, her eyes kept popping open. And Cassie was taking off her immaculate star-shaped glasses and unnecessarily polishing them on the hem of her gauzy silver shirt for what was at least the fourth time. Upside-down Astra, who could effort-lessly walk on her hands through an obstacle course with her eyes closed, had just clumsily bumped into Clover. This caused Clover, who was juggling three ozziefruits, to drop the fruit to the floor. Tessa absentmindedly picked one up and took a big bite. "Tessa!" snapped the usually starmazingly patient Clover. Tessa turned to her, her lips darkened by the indigo juice. "Sorry," she said. "I get even hungrier than usual when I'm worried." Clover looked like she was going to say something else, then picked up a substitute glorange from a bowl on the table.

But instead of returning to juggling, she sighed and sat down next to Leona, who was fiddling around with her microphone. These girls needed a distraction, and fast.

Gemma knew she was a talker. A chirpy, cheerful chatterbox. Gaps in conversation seemed empty and uncomfortable to her. Why stand there in uneasy silence when she could fill it with a joke, an interesting observation, or just some friendly chitchat? She had a lot to say about everything—and anything—under the suns, and she always had the confidence to speak up and state what was on her mind. It puzzled her to no end that this ability of hers could occasionally irritate those around her. (It was her observation that those who did not appreciate her ability generally had a lot less to say than she did or were lacking the confidence to speak up.) Gemma knew that her talkativeness could come in quite handy for her classmates. When Cassie, who could be very quiet, got called on unexpectedly in class and blushed a stunning shade of silver, Gemma would helpfully offer an opinion to give her a moment to gather her thoughts. And during those awkward lulls in conversation among acquaintances, when everyone was standing around, looking at their feet, searching for something to talk about, Gemma always knew exactly what to say. If she didn't, she made something up.

"You have the gift of gab, my starshine," her grandmother used to tell her. That was exactly how Gemma saw it, as a great gift. And now it was time to bestow that gift upon her fellow Star Darlings. With everyone about to go supernova with edginess, she felt in her heart of hearts that it was her job to make them all feel at ease. Plus, she thought she might burst if she didn't start talking again. The silence felt even more oppressive and heavy to her that day.

With a quick glance at Adora, Gemma opened her mouth, about to launch into some pleasant, distracting chatter. But just then she felt a slight tremble in her fingers as a message arrived in her Star-Zap's in-box. Her pulse quickened. This was it! As the phone began to chime and flash, there was a collective sharp intake of breath. Gemma squeezed her eyes shut for a split starsec, then opened them and read the words on-screen aloud to the group: HOLO-MESSAGE DECLINED.

Gemma's heart sank. The downcast faces of the other Star Darlings mirrored exactly what she felt. Disappointed. Scared. Guilty.

"This is terrible," Gemma said. "It means that Lady Stella has not forgiven us." She felt her face getting hot and she knew that her cheeks were probably bright orange. This was their fault! If only they hadn't turned on Lady Stella, she'd have been with them right then and there.

Sage looked sad. "We made a mistake," she said. "We took the evidence we were presented with and we made a decision—a bad one." But then she straightened up and spoke almost fiercely. "But we can fix it. I'm sure we can. We are the twelve Star-Charmed Starlings, aren't we?"

A few of the girls shook their heads. "Clearly she doesn't want to talk to us," said Tessa. "Not that I can blame her."

"Wait a minute," said Astra. "You mean you think that Lady Stella wouldn't accept our message? I'm thinking that it means she didn't receive it."

Clover nodded her head in agreement. "I don't think she's blocking us. If she was, it would have read 'sender rejected.'"

There was silence as they all tried not to look at each other, wondering why anyone would have seen fit to block a message from lovely Clover. But she wasn't offering an explanation. Perhaps that was a story for another starday.

Piper stood, her seafoam-green eyes misty and

faraway-looking. "Maybe Lady Stella isn't angry with us at all. Maybe . . . possibly . . . she needs our help. . . ." Her voice trailed off and she sat down abruptly.

Gemma stared. Sometimes Piper said things that were so odd that everyone just ignored them. But maybe there was something to that thought. . . .

"Our message probably just didn't go through," said Sage. "Otherwise we would have gotten her outgoing message. Like this." She stood, holding out her Star-Zap. A hologram of her mother, clad in a lavender cape, popped up. "I'm sorry," her holo-self said, "but I am away on a business trip and cannot be reached. Please try again." Even in hologram form Indirra was beautiful, an older and taller version of Sage with the same large violet eyes, pointy chin, and lavender hair.

"You're right," said Vega. "Lady Stella's Star-Zap should have an outgoing message." She peered more closely at Sage, who looked uneasy. "Is something wrong?"

Sage took a deep breath. "I know I shouldn't be worried," she said. "But I am. It's very unusual that my mom's message would come up for me. In the past, even on her most classified business trips, calls from the family would go through. This just doesn't feel right to me."

Cassie stood to put a comforting hand on Sage's

shoulder and Gemma noticed that it seemed to almost instantly calm the girl. Sage thought for a moment and brightened.

"Hey, I have an idea!" she announced. "We should go tell Lady Cordial the good news. She's been such a mess trying to hold this place together. I mean, it took her star ages to figure out how to start conserving energy on campus. And now she's totally fixated on planning Starshine Day when it's obvious it needs to be postponed so we can spend our time concentrating on coming up with new and better ways to save energy. I'm positive this will be a big relief to her."

"I like that idea," said Gemma, Piper's words disappearing from her mind. "I think that will make Lady Cordial feel so much better." Poor Lady Cordial. She simply wasn't headmistress material, and she had been thrust into the role after the disappearance of Lady Stella. She was obviously trying her best, but that wasn't cutting the ballum blossom sauce.

"Shall we go now?" asked Sage.

"Sure," said Leona, jumping to her feet. Gemma watched as Leona casually reached down to grab Scarlet's hand and hoisted her up. Sage pulled open the door, and she, Astra, and Leona led the way as the rest of the girls fell into place behind them, Gemma and Piper taking up the rear. They stepped on the Cosmic Transporter and Gemma half expected it to start moving them along, as it usually did. But the power to all nonessential machinery had been cut after students had begun to protest Starling Academy's wasteful wish energy practices during the crisis. Now Bot-Bots were set in sleep mode unless absolutely necessary, food choices were limited in the Celestial Café (much to Tessa's chagrin), and doors needed to be opened manually, to name but a few changes.

CONSERVE WISH ENERGY: LEVITATE OBJECTS ONLY WHEN ABSOLUTELY NECESSARY, a flickering holo-sign read. Another proclaimed SPARKLE SHOWER WITH A FRIEND, and showed two smiling Starlings showering in bathing suits. That one made Gemma laugh, as it was intended to. A little Starlandian humor in the face of an overwhelming situation.

Gemma turned to Piper. "This is good," she said. "I bet Lady Cordial will help us find Lady Stella now that we know she can be trusted. Those two have been working together for a while now and seemed very close. Lady Cordial could have an idea of where to find Lady Stella."

"Mmmmm-hmmm," replied Piper distractedly. In the bright sunlight, her dulled appearance was more apparent to Gemma. She didn't even want to see her own reflection. Sparkle shower rationing made everyone dimmer and less vibrant. It was disheartening.

The girls pushed open the heavy doors to Halo Hall. The starmarble corridors, usually crowded and bustling, were empty and quiet on this Babsday, the second day of the Starlandian weekend. Gemma even missed the roaming Bot-Bot guards, which she realized gave her a sense of security. The Star Darlings' footfalls echoed ominously in the empty hallways, which suddenly seemed full of looming shadows.

"This is weird," Gemma whispered to Piper, who stared straight ahead, not acknowledging that she had been spoken to.

Apparently the rest of the group felt the same. They had been chattering excitedly on the walk to Halo Hall, but suddenly their voices were silenced. Wordlessly, they walked to Lady Stella's old office. Leona raised her hand to knock, but Sage boldly slid the door open and stepped inside.

The rest of the girls filed in behind her. Gemma was right behind Piper, who slowed for a starmin.

Piper turned and grabbed Gemma. Her fingers felt icy cold on Gemma's bare arm. "Should we be doing this?" she blurted out. Her eyes seemed clouded and her brow was furrowed. "I—I'm just not sure about this." She bit her lip. "Maybe it will just confuse Lady Cordial more. Maybe we should handle this on our own."

Gemma considered that. But the girls were energized and positive for the first time in a while. It felt good to be doing something, taking action. And they were already there, for stars' sake. She shrugged. "It probably can't hurt," she said.

"Okay," said Piper, though she still looked a bit doubtful. She turned and glided through the doorway. With a deep breath, Gemma stepped inside and pulled the door shut behind them.

CHAPTER 2

"Halt! Who goes there?" shouted a robotic voice. Gemma felt a jolt of fear and jumped.

"We-we're looking for Lady Cordial," said Sage in an unexpectedly shaky tone. Clearly the Bot-Bot voice had startled her, too.

A shiny Bot-Bot zoomed toward them from a dark corner of the room, its eyes blinking and its voice loud and commanding. "State your purpose, Starlings," the Bot-Bot said.

Leona spoke up. "We need to talk to Lady Cordial," she said. Her eyes narrowed as she stared at the floating robot. "I thought all Bot-Bots were in sleep mode until further notice. What's going on?"

"Not guard Bot-Bots," said the Bot-Bot. "My job is to protect Lady Cordial's office at all times."

"Lady Stella's office," Clover muttered under her breath. "It will always be Lady Stella's office." Gemma silently agreed.

"Well, where is she?" asked Sage impatiently, having regained her composure. "We have some important news to tell her."

"Lady Cordial is on her way to address the student body," the Bot-Bot said in its clipped tone, "at the assembly."

"At what assembly?" said Gemma just as the Star Darlings' Star-Zaps all started vibrating. Looking down, Gemma saw that they had just received a school-wide holo-blast: GATHER IMMEDIATELY AT THE BAND SHELL FOR A QUICK UPDATE ON STARSHINE DAY FROM YOUR HEADMISTRESS. STARPRISE GUEST ENTERTAINMENT!

"Maybe she's going to announce that she's postponing Starshine Day until the energy shortage is fixed," Cassie suggested reasonably. "That would make sense."

"Does Lady Cordial ever make sense?" scoffed Leona. It was an unkind thing to say, but there was some merit to it. Lady Cordial was, in the best of situations, nervous and awkward. With Lady Stella away, she seemed to be making bad decision after bad decision.

The girls made their way to the band shell and plopped themselves down on the stargrassy area in front of the stage. They watched as the Star Quad began to fill with students. Some had brought blankets, which they spread on the ground, while others stood around, chatting with fellow students. The overall mood seemed to be slight puzzlement at the last-minute invitation, but pleasure nonetheless at being outside with friends. The sun was shining brightly and there was a slight breeze, which felt refreshing. Gemma closed her eyes and lifted her face to the sun, knowing the result would be a smattering of light orange star-shaped freckles across her nose. She caught snippets of conversations, which mostly seemed to be about news from home—Starcarpool regulations, newly added HOS lanes, and sparkle shower rationing. That made Gemma realize that she hadn't heard a star news report on campus in a while—or, come to think of it, seen a copy of a holo-newspaper. Very odd.

"What in the stars?" she heard Leona say. Gemma's eyes snapped open. Leona was pointing to the stage. A girl with a bright green aura was dragging out a drum kit. Leona stood, walked onto the stage, and started talking to the girl in green. Another girl, in a pale blue robe, hurried out to join them. It looked like Leona and the new girl got into a discussion that was not particularly friendly. Gemma watched as Leona turned, her face angry, and stormed off.

Scarlet, who had been lying on her back, staring up at the clouds, raised her head. "Where did Leona go?" she asked. Gemma shrugged and closed her eyes again. Vega was deep in a holo–crossword puzzle and Piper was, of course, meditating. Truth be told, Gemma didn't care if the assembly ever started. It was nice to just empty her mind and relax, to not think about anything. It had been far too long since she'd had the pleasure of doing that.

Just then Cassie grabbed Gemma's arm and Gemma snapped her eyes open. Lady Cordial was standing in the middle of the stage, staring out at the crowd. The students watched as she took a deep breath and pulled a purple microphone out of one of her voluminous pockets. Lady Cordial's face was pale and she looked as ill at ease as ever. "It's painful to watch," muttered Cassie, who knew a thing or two about feeling awkward. It was obvious that the responsibility that had been thrust upon Lady Cordial due to Lady Stella's abrupt depar- ture hadn't done a thing to boost her self-confidence. Someone jostled Gemma as she sat down next to her. Gemma gave a sidelong glance and realized it was Leona. The Starling didn't look angry anymore, and she was grinning wickedly. But before Gemma could ask what Leona was up to, Lady Cordial began to speak.

"S-s-s-star greetings, s-s-s-students," she said softly into the microphone. The students continued to talk. She raised her voice and tried again. "S-s-s-star greetings, s-s-s-students," she repeated, and the crowd began to quiet down. "As you all know, S-s-s-starland is in a bit of an energy crisis. Belts have been tightened and we are now doing all we can to help conserve energy on campus. And don't think I haven't noticed the s-s-s-sacrifices that you have all made! You deserve to be commended! S-s-s-so with Lady S-s-s-stella s-s-s-still temporarily away, I have made the executive decision to keep S-s-s-starshine Day on the calendar, which, as you know, is coming up s-s-s-soon. This is an important celebration for us all and I am counting on all of you to pitch in to make this a resounding s-s-s-success. It will boost morale and foster feelings of hope and camaraderie among s-s-s-students and faculty alike."

The Star Darlings glanced at one another. Was she serious? Starshine Day was still going to happen despite all the uncertainty?

"The S-s-s-starshine Day committee has been hard at work, but now we must ask for your help to make this day go off without a hitch. In a few s-s-s-starsecs you will each receive an assignment on your S-s-s-star-Zaps."

Gemma's Star-Zap vibrated and she looked down. The screen read DECORATING COMMITTEE. She glanced over Tessa's shoulder. FOOD COMMITTEE. Figured. Astra was on the games committee, and Leona was entertainment. The other girls were assigned to hospitality, science fair, prizes, sports, animals, light shows, art fair, costumes, and the parade. Oddly, none of the Star Darlings were on the same committee.

"Are there any questions?" Lady Cordial asked after the general post-assignment hubbub died down.

Several arms shot up, including Sage's and Astra's. But Lady Cordial didn't notice. She squinted at the crowd and said, "Okay then, let's go s-s-s-straight to the entertainment! As you know, we will be having an exciting Battle of the Bands competition on S-s-s-starshine Day, with a gift certificate from Musical Madness for the winners! Today we have a s-s-s-special treat. Competitors Vivica and the Visionaries are going to give you a preview of their s-s-s-spectacular s-s-s-sound!"

The crowd clapped politely as Vivica and her bandmates ran onstage. They were all in sparkly outfits that matched their auras, and Gemma had to admit that

Vivica's light blue outfit, which looked like it was made of moonbeams, was positively stellar. As the drummer, keyboardist, and guitarist got into position, Vivica raised the mic to her lips. "Hey, everyone, I'm Vivica," she said, pointing to herself, "and these"—she pointed to her band—"are the Visionaries. And we're here to get you pumped for Starshine Day. We're gonna rock your star-socks off! The song we're going to sing is the brand-new anthem 'Starshine Day Is Coming.' It's a song written and composed by our very own headmistress, Lady Cordial. It's a great song that I am sure you will enjoy, and . . ."

As Vivica went on (and on), Leona turned to Gemma and placed something in her hand. Gemma looked down and blinked at the star-shaped orange devices. "Ear shields?" she said. "Really, Leona?"

Leona grinned. "I ran into Vivica onstage when I went up to check out the drum kit. She was so rude and called us embarrassing amateurs! Of all the nerve! So I ran off to the star emporium to pick up twelve pairs." She gave Gemma a pleading look. "Come on, put them on. It's just a little joke!"

Gemma bit her lip. "I don't know," she said. "Aren't we supposed to rise above others' petty behavior?"

Leona did not look at all convinced, so Gemma tried another tactic. "Don't you want to hear what the competition sounds like?" she asked.

"Nope," said Leona. "I've heard them play one too many times already."

"Maybe *I* want to hear them," said Gemma.

"Come on," begged Leona. "Humor me!"

"Fine," said Gemma with a sigh. She held them tightly in her hand as she watched Leona hand out the ear shields to rest of the Star Darlings. Some questioned her, but most of the girls just shrugged and placed them over their ears. Donning ear shields at a performance was an aggressive move, especially when your rival was onstage.

Gemma held off, curious to hear a bit of the music before sealing up her ears. Vivica turned to the band and said, "A-one, a-two, a-one, two, three . . ." and the Visionaries burst into song:

Starshine Day is coming
Time to celebrate
Starshine Day is coming
Hurry, don't be late

Not too bad, actually, thought Gemma. The tune was bright and bouncy, and Vivica, surprisingly, had a clear, sweet voice. Gemma suddenly felt startacularly excited about Starshine Day and started clapping along to the music. But after a sharp elbow to the ribs and a look of disapproval from Leona, she reluctantly fastened the ear shields over her ears. She was immediately engulfed in silence. It was a strange experience, almost like being underwater. She could see girls in the audience mouthing the lyrics, dancing, and jumping up and down. But because she couldn't hear anything at all, she felt like she was watching everything from a distance. The crowd had certainly perked up. She looked all around her. They really appeared to be enjoying the music. One girl even looked like she was about to cry with joy!

Leona, standing next to Gemma, jostled her arm. Gemma glanced over and saw Leona remove something from her pocket. She took a closer look. It was black and misshapen, but Leona cradled it in her hand quite lovingly. Suddenly, Gemma realized what it was—Leona's ruined Wish Pendant, a cuff bracelet, once gleaming and golden. Poor Leona! Gemma felt very sad for her friend and her dashed dreams. Leona would never get a Wish Blossom or a Power Crystal. The ruined accessory was a reminder of that. If Gemma were Leona, she'd just throw it away. Who needed a token of one's failure?

Gemma realized that Vivica and the Visionaries had finished playing as they took a bow and exited the stage. She removed her ear shields and put them in her pocket. The crowd wasn't moving, apparently hoping that the band would come back and sing some more. They lingered for quite a while. When it was clear that the band wouldn't be playing another song, the crowd reluctantly began to disperse.

Leona smiled at the other Star Darlings. "Star salutations for humoring me," she said. Scarlet gave her a look that Gemma could only translate to "I can't believe you asked us to do that" and possibly "I'm shocked that we all agreed," and Leona rolled her warm golden eyes back at her roommate. "And yes, Scarlet, I do know that I was being childish."

Gemma shrugged. It was no big deal. "You're welcome," she said. She was about to say more when she spotted Lolo, a girl who had a turquoise aura and was in her lighterature class, passing by. Gemma reached out an arm and stopped her. The girl blinked at her sleepily, as if she had just woken up.

"Hey, Lolo," Gemma said. "I was wondering if I could borrow your notes from yesterday's class. I can't find mine anywhere. It's like they disappeared."

Lolo smiled at Gemma as if she hadn't heard a word she had said. "What a startastic song," she said. "I'm so excited that Starshine Day is coming."

Gemma frowned. "But don't you think it's weird that we're still celebrating Starshine Day even though we're in the middle of an energy shortage?"

The girl looked back at her blankly. "No," she said, shaking her head. "Not at all. Starshine Day is coming."

A girl with bright pink curls springing out from under a knit cap stopped in her tracks. "Oh, yes," she gushed. "Starshine Day is going to be startacular!"

Passing girls began saying, "Starshine Day! Starshine Day!" until, to Gemma's starprise, it became a chant. Gemma turned to the rest of the Star Darlings, who still stood in front of the stage in a tight little group.

Clover's piercing purple eyes flashed. "Did you know that Starshine Day is coming?" she said sarcastically.

"So I've heard," said Gemma. "What's going on?"

"We're waiting for Lady Cordial," answered Clover. "We're going to tell her the news about Lady Stella."

"Startastic. That'll put an end to all this Starshine Day silliness," Gemma said.

Clover nodded in agreement.

Just then Lady Cordial emerged from backstage,

flanked by two Bot-Bots. She stepped off the stage and hurried past the Star Darlings, so focused on her Star-Zap that she appeared not to notice them.

"Lady Cordial!" called Astra. The headmistress turned and stopped.

"Hold it right there," said one of the Bot-Bots.

"At ease, RE-D7," said Lady Cordial. "You may proceed, girls."

Sage opened her mouth to speak, but Leona burst out with "Vivica and the Visionaries? Really?"

"Leona!" said Scarlet warningly.

Lady Cordial's eyes glittered and Gemma was afraid for a moment that Leona had angered her. But then her expression changed. "S-s-s-star apologies," she said. "But Vivica begged for a chance to practice in front of a crowd. It was thoughtless of me. Thoughtless."

Leona made a face and folded her arms tightly across her chest. "Fine," she said, though Gemma could tell she was still steaming. "We'll beat them fair and square. You'll see," she said, her words clipped.

"Is that all, girls?" asked Lady Cordial. "There's s-s-s-so much to do to get ready!"

"Actually, we have some great news to tell you," Gemma said.

"Great news!" echoed Libby.

"The very best!" said Cassie.

Sage and Astra both opened their mouths to speak, but Gemma felt like she was going to burst if she didn't say something. "We're pretty certain that Lady Stella is not the culprit!" she blurted.

Lady Cordial looked shocked. Then her expression grew soft with sadness. "Oh, you poor, poor girls," she said. "This is a very difficult s-s-s-situation for you. You're quite clearly in denial about Lady S-s-s-stella's involvement. Completely understandable."

Sage pushed forward. "Actually, we're almost a hydrong percent sure of it. We recently discovered that Lady Stella has been consulting with my mother," she explained. "You know, Indirra, the top wish energy scientist? So Lady Stella is clearly working with her on a solution to the shortage. She's not the one sabotaging us."

"Well, how do you explain that all the terrible things s-s-s-stopped as s-s-s-soon as she disappeared?" Lady Cordial asked.

"We're convinced it was a coincidence," said Cassie. "Or maybe the real saboteur stopped as soon as Lady Stella disappeared to make her look guilty."

Lady Cordial considered this. "I guess that's possible. . . ."

Gemma piped up. "It's such a relief to know she's on our side," she said. "We were all so worried!"

Lady Cordial opened her mouth to speak, then shut it just as quickly. She took a deep breath and appeared to be thinking. "Of course. How wonderful to hear this news. Did you also find out if she'll be returning s-s-s-soon?" she asked eagerly.

The Star Darlings' faces fell. "We . . . um . . . thought that you might be able to help us with that," Gemma explained. "We can't seem to find her."

Lady Cordial shook her head. "I'm s-s-s-sorry, girls," she said, "but I have no idea where she could be." She smiled at them. "Well, keep me posted," she said. "This is exciting news indeed!"

"So will we postpone Starshine Day?" Gemma asked.

Lady Cordial looked at her as if she had two auras. "Postpone S-s-s-starshine Day?" she said, her eyes wide. "On the contrary! We must s-s-s-step up the preparations in honor of Lady S-s-s-stella's return. This c-c-celebration is even more important than ever!"

CHAPTER
3

Starshine Day, Starshine Day. That was all anyone could talk about after Lady Cordial's impromptu
assembly. The Star Darlings were getting tired of hearing about it. Students and teachers discussed it in class.
They received holo-reminders about it every starday. It
was talked about in the echoing starmarble hallways of
Halo Hall, at the finely set tables in the Celestial Café,
and on the soft, comfortable couches in the Lightning
Lounge. It seemed that everyone, except for the Star
Darlings, had Starshine Day on the brain.

It was last period on Yumday, and the Star Darlings
had assembled in their secret classroom, waiting for
the guest lecturer to arrive. They were hoping it would
be Lady Cordial. There were so many unanswered

questions: Was there anything they could do to help with the shortage? Did Lady Cordial have any further thoughts about where Lady Stella could be? Could she offer them any help in trying to figure out who the saboteur was now that Lady Stella was no longer their number one suspect? And did she have any idea when the twelfth and final Wish Orb would reveal itself?

"I just don't remember Starshine Day being such a big deal last year," Adora was saying as they waited. "I mean, it's a fun day and all, don't get me wrong. I always have a great time and I especially enjoy the interactive science experiment exhibit. But this is a little over the stars, don't you think?"

"Totally," Clover replied. "Especially since we're in the middle of this energy shortage." The rest of the Star Darlings nodded in agreement.

"So what are the chances that our guest lecturer makes an appearance today?" Libby said as she twisted a strand of jellyjooble-pink hair around her finger.

Vega perked up. Now they were speaking her language. "Oh, I'd say it's one in—"

"It might as well be one in ten moonium," interrupted Scarlet in a bored voice. She was sprawled on the floor with her head leaning against the wall, tapping her big clunky boots together rhythmically. "Face it, Vega, no one's coming. We haven't had Star Darlings class in stardays. We keep showing up, but the guest lecturer never does. It's like everyone forgot about us or something. I say we shouldn't waste our time."

"Oooh," said Leona. "That's really bad. You mean, you think everyone has given up on the Star Darlings?"

Gemma grew irritated. She didn't like the sound of that at all.

Piper spoke up and her voice startled Gemma. "Maybe it's because we already know everything there is to know about being a Star Darling," she offered. "Maybe it's actually a star compliment!"

"Maybe," said Gemma. But she didn't really believe that. "Actually, I'm worried about my Wish Orb. When will it be ready?" Maybe Lady Cordial was too distracted by her duties and responsibilities and had lost sight of the importance of the final Wish Orb. Gemma desperately wanted to be sent to Wishworld. (She didn't want to say it out loud, but she was wondering if her Wish Mission—the twelfth and final one—could be the mission that would collect enough energy to save Starland, which she believed would fulfill the prophecy.) Then she had a scary thought and was seized with panic. Maybe

Lady Cordial knew something they didn't know. Maybe there wasn't going to be a Wish Orb for her at all.

"Let's try Lady Stella again," Cassie suggested. "We just have to keep sending messages until we reach her."

But the result was the same: HOLO-MESSAGE DECLINED. The looks on the girls' faces ranged from disappointed to sullen, teary to fed up.

Sage shook her head. "I haven't gotten through to my mother, either, but Dad and Gran keep telling me she's fine, not to worry. Of course, they have no idea about what's going on with Lady Stella."

Gemma wished she had the right words to help take the worried look out of Sage's lavender eyes. She was about to start trying when the bell rang for the end of class. Scarlet stood up and brushed off her black tulle skirt with hot-pink lining. She grinned wickedly and hopped up on the desk, where she perched primly. "Students, class dismissed!" she called out in a perfect imitation of Professor Lucretia Delphinus. "I hope you all enjoyed my fascinating lecture on the different types of Wish Pendant glows, though I did notice a few of you nodding off in the middle of my discussion of faintly bright versus somewhat bright, which could be considered quite rude! But perhaps you were overwhelmed by the sheer volume of information I provided today. Now if someone could just help me get down from this desk . . . Is there a Flash Vertical Mover around here?"

"Scarlet!" said Piper, shaking her head reproachfully. "Be nice!" But even she couldn't help smiling. Scarlet's imitation of the tough and tiny teacher had been starspot-on.

"Off to our Starshine Day committees," said Tessa with a sigh. "As usual." All after-school clubs, meetings, and sports had been put on hold until after Starshine Day so students and faculty could fully concentrate on the preparations, per Lady Cordial's direct orders. Her laser-sharp focus on this one event was troubling to Gemma, who wondered why Lady Cordial didn't seem concerned about who had been sabotaging them (since Lady Stella had been cleared), the shortage, or the delinquent Wish Orb. She'd ask her all those questions if she got the chance.

She waved to the other Star Darlings as the girls went their separate ways to their various committees and Gemma headed to her own—the decorating committee, which was made up of a group of students who were all startastically excited to have such a big part in making Starshine Day "the best it could be," plus Gemma.

"Star greetings, Gemma!" called a girl named Tansy.
"It's so nice to see you this starday." Tansy had a sweet
round face and a pale pink aura. Gemma smiled despite
herself; the girl was so kind and gentle she deserved
a warm greeting in return, no matter how grumpy
Gemma might be feeling. "Star greetings, Tansy," she
said as she settled into the stargrass next to her. They
had been tasked with stringing what felt like floozels
of briteflower garlands, which they would hang all
over campus. Gemma picked up a half-strung garland
and, with a sigh, began threading the small twinkling
white blossoms onto it by hand, one by one. Every task,
every preparation these days took an agonizingly long
time, as everything needed to be done the old-fashioned
way, which was the way many things were done on
Wishworld—by hand.

Gemma's thoughts wandered back to her Wish
Mission and she pricked her finger with the needle.
"Ouch!" she cried. If this was what life was like on
Wishworld every starday, she had no idea why Scarlet
wanted to live there so badly. Everything was so much
harder without the hands-free benefits of utilizing wish
energy. But the rest of the girls laughed and sang as they
worked and seemed so happy to be there. They never
complained that they were bored or that their fingers

hurt. They didn't seem to have a care in the world. *Why are they so excited about Starshine Day and I'm not?* Gemma wondered.

By the middle of the starweek Gemma felt more irritable than ever. Each and every one of her fingers was sore. And every time her Star-Zap vibrated, she snatched it up, hoping to find a message about Lady Stella or the Wish Orb. But it was always a useless Starshine Day update from Lady Cordial. And while the temporary headmistress was in constant communication via her Star-Zap, she was nowhere to be seen.

The hydrongs of briteflower garlands were finally done, and it was time to begin the arduous task of hanging them. Since the Starlings couldn't use their wish energy manipulation to effortlessly fasten the garlands, someone managed to find an ancient ladder from the old days and dragged it out. They carried it over to the first lamppost, set it up, and then stared at the contraption warily. It looked rickety and unstable and no one wanted to climb it. Tansy finally took a deep breath and ascended shakily to the top. Another girl produced an old-fashioned tool kit. Gemma rooted around in it until she found a sparklehammer and a solar-metal spike (both of which she was vaguely familiar with from the toolshed on the farm) and handed them to Tansy, who looked at the tools in confusion. "I . . . I'm not sure what to do," she said. Gemma took pity on the Starling and motioned for her to climb down, switching places with her. When she reached the top, she looked down—she was pretty far off the ground—and got a bit dizzy. She wasn't quite sure how to position the spike so she wouldn't smash her finger with the sparklehammer, but then, after some adjusting, she figured out the correct angle and did the job. *There!* She climbed back down and took a look. Her proud moment was cut short as the briteflower garland promptly fluttered to the ground.

Gemma sighed and climbed back up the ladder. From her vantage point she saw a passing Bot-Bot. They were programmed to help with all sorts of issues around Starling Academy, so she waved and called it over.

"Star greetings," she said as it got closer.

"Star greetings, I am JR-Y6," the Bot-Bot said.

"Would you help us hang this garland for Starshine Day, JR-Y6?" Gemma asked politely.

"Negative. I am currently solely in guard mode," said the Bot-Bot. "My directive is to serve Lady Cordial. I am not programmed to help you." He nodded briskly and zoomed off.

"*Starf!*" said Gemma. With a shrug, she climbed back to the top of the ladder and hammered in the spike again. To her relief, this time it stayed put.

She climbed down, carried the ladder to the second post, and climbed back up. She carefully positioned the garland, admiring it as it hung between the two posts, twinkling prettily. She was just about to pound in the spike when she spotted JR-Y6 heading off in the distance. That was when she realized that if a guard was around, Lady Cordial must not be too far away. Without hesitating, she put down the sparklehammer, jumped down from the ladder, and took off after the Bot-Bot.

"Gemma, wait!" called Tansy. It was only then that Gemma realized she was still holding on to the end of the briteflower garland. As she ran, the other end of it ripped off the first pole, scattering blossoms every which way.

"Star apologies, Tansy!" she called. "I won't be long at all."

The girl looked distraught. "But Starshine Day is coming!" she said.

Don't I know it, thought Gemma. "I'll be back soon! I promise!"

Gemma followed the guard all the way to the ozzie-fruit orchard, where it set off on a winding path through the trees. Eventually, to her astonishment, she discovered Lady Cordial sitting on a bench, about to bite into a star-sandwich, a fine picnic lunch spread out around her.

"Oh, Gemma!" Lady Cordial cried, jumping up to greet her. Gemma grimaced as the fine china plate that had been sitting on her lap smashed into smithereens on the stone walkway. "Oh, dear," Lady Cordial said sheepishly. "How clumsy of me."

Two Bot-Bot guards zoomed closer, then hovered nearby. To Gemma's starprise, one of them winked at her. Gemma realized it was MO-J4, otherwise known as Mojo—Sage's special Bot-Bot friend. She winked back.

"How can I help you, my dear?" Lady Cordial asked as the smashed china and lost star-sandwich disappeared, as messes always did on Starland.

"I need to talk to you," said Gemma. "I am feeling this tremendous pull to go to Wishworld, but my Wish Orb is still not ready." She looked up at the headmistress searchingly. "Or is it? Have you checked?"

"Every day," said Lady Cordial earnestly. "I'm just as anxious as you are. But I have this feeling, this very s-s-s-strong feeling, that we are all worrying and getting upset for no reason. I can't shake this feeling that everything is going to turn out exactly the way it is s-s-s-supposed to. And I also have this feeling, a premonition almost"—she leaned closer to Gemma, as if she was about to tell her a secret—"that it's *your* mission that will turn the tide for S-s-s-starland. That you, my dear, will be the one to return S-s-s-starland to the way it should be."

Gemma gasped and felt a glimmer of hope in her chest. "Do you really think so?" she asked eagerly. "That's exactly what I was hoping for!"

"I do," said Lady Cordial. "Just you wait and s-s-s-see. We just need to be patient." She closed her eyes, concentrated for a moment, and nodded. "Yes," she said, "I think it will all work out just in time for S-s-s-starshine Day."

"But that's only three days away!" Gemma said anxiously. She had a sudden realization. "So that means I'll be sent down on my mission any day now?"

Lady Cordial nodded. "It's almost ready, I'm sure of it," she agreed. "So rest up and s-s-s-start getting ready for the mission of a lifetime!"

Gemma walked back to the dorm in a daze, completely forgetting about Tansy and the decorating committee. She had to mentally prepare herself for this most crucial mission. Her mind was racing. *I'll keep this news to myself,* she thought. *No need to discuss it until it actually happens.* Yes, it would be good for her to sit on the information and digest it slowly. Everyone would know soon enough, at the Wish Orb reveal. She was pleased with herself for coming to that conclusion, which she felt showed great maturity and composure.

She bumped into her sister just outside of the dormitories.

"Hey, Gemma," said Tessa.

"I'mgoingonamission!" Gemma nearly shouted, all in a rush.

"Slow down," said Tessa. "Say that again?"

Oh, starf, there goes maturity and composure, Gemma thought. She looked around furtively to make sure no one had overheard, and repeated her message. "I'm going on a mission! Any day now. Lady Cordial just told me."

Tessa bit her lip.

"What's wrong?" said Gemma. "It's what we've been waiting for. This is good news for me—and for Starland."

"It's great news for Starland," Tessa replied slowly. "You, I'm not so sure. I'm worried. The last thing Mom said to me before we left for Starling Academy was that I should always look out for you."

"Really?" said Gemma. "She told me I should always look out for *you.*"

The two girls laughed. That was just like their mother—trying to make them both feel useful and trusted (and carefully looked after, of course).

"But seriously, Gemma," said Tessa, "we're having a crisis. Things keep going wrong. Adora's mission nearly was ruined because her secret Starling identity was compromised. It all turned out okay in the end, but it could have been a disaster. Not to mention Leona's messed-up mission. She almost didn't make it home."

"I'll be careful, Sis. I promise," said Gemma. "But I've got to go on this mission. The fate of Starland is hanging in the balance, you know."

"And on that dramatic note," said Tessa, "I've got to go. I'll see you later."

She turned and made a glitterbeeline toward her dorm.

"Wait a minute, where are you going?" Gemma cried. She had been hoping they could pick a few outfits together with the Wishworld Outfit Selector.

"Why, to my room, of course," Tessa called back over her shoulder. "To bake. You can't go to Wishworld without the proper amount of snacks, now can you?"

CHAPTER
4

It was a full starday later and there was still no message from Lady Cordial about Gemma's Wish Orb. So, as usual, the twelve girls assembled in the Star Darlings classroom. This time, anticipating the free hour they would most likely have, they decided they had no choice but to start preparing for the Battle of the Bands. They brought in their musical instruments, sewing supplies, and what seemed like mooniums of sequins, especially created by Adora, which they would sew onto their outfits—a striking golden pantsuit for Leona, its legs wide and flowing; a pink minidress with enormous bell sleeves for Libby; a flowy purple tunic over leggings for Sage; a bright blue bolero jacket and matching shorts for Vega; and a hooded black sweatshirt dress for Scarlet.

Gemma's sewing skills had improved dramatically after her experience with the briteflower garlands, and she chose to work on Scarlet's dress, adding hot-pink sequins to the dark material. It was going to look startastic when she finished. The only way to do it without wish energy was to pull a needle and thread through the center of each sequin, thread a tiny bead onto the needle, then push it back through the sequin, knotting the thread on the other side—over and over and over again. It was time-consuming, mindless work, but Gemma was finding it to be oddly soothing. It helped to calm her nerves. She was both bursting with excitement and trembling with apprehension, an uneasy combination. Being nervous made her chattier than ever. It soothed her a bit to keep up a constant stream of words, which she was sure entertained the other Star Darlings as they sewed on sequins, too. Meanwhile, the Star Darlings band members rehearsed. The room had been soundproofed to keep their special lessons private, so they didn't have to worry that they would be disturbing any classes while they rocked out.

After a while, the band took a break. Leona took the time to try to reach Lady Stella. Gemma held her breath as Leona holo-dialed, but there was no answer. Again.

Gemma turned to Sage, intending to ask if she had

heard from her mother. Cassie, sensing her question, shook her head and leaned over to whisper to Gemma. "No word yet," she said. "And when she last spoke to her grandmother and her father, she could have sworn that they sounded a little worried. But they assured her that everything was fine."

With break time over, Vega, Sage, and Libby picked up their instruments and Scarlet settled in behind her drums.

"Let's take that one from the top again," said Leona. "We have to be totally perfect." She looked determined. "I just *have* to beat Vivica."

Scarlet reached over and poked her in the side with a drumstick.

Leona jumped. "Oh, sorry. I mean the *Star Darlings* just have to beat Vivica and the Visionaries," she said, correcting herself.

Scarlet nodded. "That's more like it," she said.

That evening, as they walked back to their dorms after dinner, Piper spoke up. "I have an idea," she said. "We've been under a lot of pressure the past few days. Anyone want to join me for a little meditation?"

It was the last thing Gemma wanted to do. She was

envisioning herself slipping on a pair of comfy pajamas, crawling under the covers, and holo-calling her two best friends from home for a chat before she fell asleep. She glued her eyes to the ground and kept walking toward the dormitory.

When none of the Star Darlings responded, Piper pressed on. "We've all been working so hard. We're under a lot of stress. Some simple meditation will work wonders. It will center us, take our minds off our worries about Lady Stella and our concerns about this ridiculous festival. We'll all sleep really well afterwards, too."

Gemma was just about to politely bow out when she glanced over and noticed the disappointed look on Piper's kind face. She mentally changed her plans for the evening.

"I'm in," she said, a note of fake cheer in her voice. Her sister, with a barely audible sigh, followed suit. And before long, each and every Star Darling was on board. No one wanted to be the one to disappoint Piper. They made a plan to go first to their rooms and put on their comfiest clothes. Half a starhour later they were all knocking on the door to Piper and Vega's room. Gemma had dressed to relax in a silky bright orange pajama set with red trim and knotted buttons, and she had pulled her hair into two pigtails (adorable, if she did say so herself). She sniffed the air appreciatively as she stepped inside, enjoying the smell of glowball incense that wafted through the air. It brought a smile to her face, reminding her of the bouquets her father would handpick to star-prise her mother. She giggled, remembering the time her mom had leaned in to sniff a blossom and had come nose to nose with a glitterbee. The fuzzy little creature had taken a starshine to her mom and became her little pet, following her all around the house and settling on her shoulder as she read holo-books in the evening. Gemma looked over at Tessa, who also had a wistful little smile on her face, and Gemma wondered if she was sharing the same memory. Thinking of her parents, alone on the farm, struggling to keep things going in the face of the energy shortage, brought a lump to Gemma's throat. How she wished that Wish Orb would just start glowing.

Gentle music was playing and Gemma could already feel the tensions of the day easing from her tight shoulders. She lowered herself to the ground to sit on a soft orange cushion. There were colorful cushions in each girl's signature color scattered on the floor, and Gemma watched as her friends sank onto theirs gratefully. They all switched their Star-Zaps to silent mode and placed them within arm's reach, just in case. Gemma looked around and smiled. The lighting was muted and very peaceful.

Piper sat facing the girls on her own seafoam-green cushion. She wore a long sleeveless tunic in varying shades of green over a pair of knit leggings. Her hair was pulled back smoothly into a rippling ponytail. She smiled at the girls, looking quite pleased to have them all there together. Gemma admired Piper for her serene demeanor. She was suddenly quite glad to be there, and she hoped that this meditation experiment might bring her some inner peace to replace the anxiety that had been troubling her.

Piper pressed her hands together and brought them to her face, bowing her head at them in greeting. "Welcome," she said. "I'm so starfully happy that you all have chosen to spend your evening with me in meditation. Through meditation we learn to become calm and at peace with ourselves. We will learn how to be more focused, how to transform our minds from negative to positive."

Sign me up! thought Gemma. *I'm ready!*

"Now we'll begin. Everyone, please sit up straight, but still make sure that you are feeling comfortable. Not quite so tense, Vega . . . no, no, oh, yes, that's much better.

Are you all sitting criss-cross starapple sauce? Perfect! Now place your hands on your knees, palms up. Close your eyes and concentrate on your breathing."

Gemma had never really thought about breathing before. It just happened; it was something you never considered. She concentrated on the action. In and out. In and out. Wait—was she breathing too fast? Or too slow? How many breaths were you supposed to take in a starmin, anyway? Were there rules for breathing that she didn't know about? She had so many questions!

"Now don't change the way you are breathing, just pay close attention to the way that you inhale and exhale," Piper said, as if she had heard Gemma's thoughts. Actually, knowing Piper's many talents, Gemma wouldn't put it past her. "Think of your chest, rising and falling with each breath. Good! Now we'll do this for two starmins."

Gemma was trying really hard to just think about her breaths, but she found her mind wandering, not to energy shortages and missing headmistresses, as she might have expected, but oddly enough to briteflower garlands. Were they sparklehammered in properly? What if the night was windy? Would they fall? Had they hung them up too soon?

Piper's soft voice sounded in her ear. "If you find

your mind wandering, get right back to your breaths. In and out, in and out." Gemma's eyes flew open, but Piper was still sitting on her cushion at the front of the room. Her words had the desired effect, nevertheless, and Gemma was once again where she needed to be, at least in terms of meditation.

Piper's voice grew more distant. "Through meditation we will learn to free ourselves from unnecessary worries and achieve peaceful minds. This is the way to experience true happiness.

"Now," she said when the two starmins of concentrated breathing were up, "we are going to introduce a mantra. This is a simple word or phrase we will concentrate on that will really help you to focus your mind. We will all think of a simple word or phrase to focus on. We will repeat this mantra silently over and over to ourselves. I'll give you a moment to choose a word or phrase." Gemma felt a slight ripple in the air as Piper passed by.

"Has everyone chosen a mantra? Now it's time to think of your word," Piper said.

"Wish Orb!" said Gemma.

"Say it in your head, just to yourself," Piper corrected gently.

"Wish Orb!" Gemma repeated.

"Shhh," said Tessa irritably next to her. Clearly, her sister needed more meditation.

"No—Wish Orb!" Gemma shouted, holding up her Star-Zap. "Everybody check your Star-Zaps! My Wish Orb is ready!"

CHAPTER
5

The room broke out into excited chattering. Finally!

Gemma's eyes were shining. "The timing is perfect!" she said. "Lady Cordial said she had a feeling that everything would be straightened out in time for Starshine Day. I just know that this mission is going to collect a starton of wish energy!" she said confidently.

As Gemma stood, she noticed that Leona, who was still sitting on her golden cushion, slipped her hand into her pocket. Gemma knew exactly what she was doing—running her fingers over her ruined Wish Pendant and thinking of her own failed mission. Gemma wanted to tell her that it was okay, that hopefully her mission would more than make up for Leona's, but she thought the girl might take it the wrong way.

Gemma was all set to sprint to Lady Cordial's office when Sage stepped in front of the door and cleared her throat. "I just want to say that while you are off on your mission, we will continue to try to locate Lady Stella. Maybe we'll find her by the time you return and we can fix this problem for good."

"I hope so," said Gemma. "Can we go now?"

Slip-slap, slip-slap. Gemma walked so quickly to Halo Hall that she almost lost an orange slipper along the way. Only Astra was able (or willing) to keep up with her. When Gemma arrived at the office door, she paused.

"Are you okay?" asked Astra.

Gemma nodded, but inside she felt paralyzed. What if her mission went wrong and she didn't collect any energy? What if something went wonky with the wish energy and she got stuck on Wishworld? That would be fine for Scarlet, but Gemma liked living on Starland! And what if the girls didn't find Lady Stella while she was gone? So many what-ifs kept crowding her mind, all of them bad. She closed her eyes, and a voice, clear and strong, suddenly cut through the chatter. It said, "Just remember these words: while looking to the future, you must not forget the past."

Gemma's hands trembled. She turned to Astra. "Did you just hear that?" she asked.

"Hear what?" Astra said.

"Um, nothing," Gemma replied. She didn't want to say anything to get Astra's hopes up, but the voice had reminded her of someone very dear to her—to all of them. It had sounded a lot like Lady Stella. Emboldened, and with the rest of the Star Darlings' footfalls sounding in the hallway, she knocked and then slid the door open.

Gemma blinked. The number of Bot-Bot guards in Lady Cordial's office had swelled to four.

"That's a lot of Bot-Bots," she remarked.

"Oh, better s-s s-safe than s-s-s sorry," Lady Cordial said offhandedly.

The rest of the Star Darlings filed into the room and took their seats around the full moon–shaped table.

"Welcome, everyone," said Lady Cordial. "I am sure you are as pleased as I am that the final Wish Orb has been identified. There's no question who it belongs to, s-s-s-so we will dispense with the dramatic reveal and s-s-s-simply open the box."

Lady Cordial reached behind the desk and produced

a large solar-metal box. She placed it on the table directly in front of Gemma. All of a sudden the sides fell away to reveal a smaller box. The wait was agonizing to Gemma as she watched this happen again and again. She kept a smile on her face, but she really just wanted to scream. Finally, there was a Wish Orb–sized box sitting in front of her.

"Open it, Gemma," said Lady Cordial.

Gemma lifted the lid, which was surprisingly light. She gasped as the orb—*her* orb—rose into the air. She blinked. Was it her imagination or was it moving a bit shakily? She reached out her hand, but the orb simply bobbed in place in front of her. She looked around. The rest of the Star Darlings were staring at the orb oddly, too.

"It looks . . . different," she said. It appeared to be much more sparkly than the other orbs, but somehow less glowing. And it was quite large and bulgy—almost like it was ready to burst.

"That's because it is the final orb. The most crucial one!" said Lady Cordial. She leaned over and whispered into Gemma's ear. "The most important mission of them all."

Gemma shivered with excitement as a tingle ran down her spine. The twelfth and final mission. The biggest one of all. It was quite an honor—and a great responsibility. She felt like making a speech to commemorate the occasion.

She continued to hold out her hand. Lady Cordial, perhaps unable to stand the suspense, bustled over and plucked the orb out of the air.

Gemma waited for Lady Cordial to place it in her hand, imagining the smooth surface against her skin, the warmth that would flood her hand and run up her arm and into her body. But Lady Cordial instead placed the orb back in the box and snapped it shut.

"Are you ready, Gemma?" she asked.

"I am," replied Gemma. "As a matter of fact, I just wanted to say a word or two about . . ." She then launched into a speech about last chances, bravery in the face of adversity, and the importance of support from one's peers. "And in conclusion—" she began.

Lady Cordial put her hands on Gemma's shoulders and squeezed, perhaps a little too tightly in Gemma's opinion. Gemma shifted uncomfortably. "S-s-s-star s-s-s-salutations for that inspiring s-s-s-speech, Gemma," Lady Cordial said. "Now it's time to prepare for the final Wish Mission. The fate of S-s-s-starland rests in your hands."

Gemma thought for a moment. As the voice had said, she had to look back into the future. She frowned. Or maybe it was that the future was in the past? In any event, her mission—the twelfth and final one—was about to start.

CHAPTER
6

By the time Gemma landed on Wishworld, her head was spinning, her hands were shaking, and her mind was racing. The trip down to Wishworld had been much more tumultuous than her previous journey, with dips and falls, near misses, and close calls. Whether an increase in negative wish energy in the atmosphere or an overabundance of solar activity was causing the disturbances, she did not know. The funny part was that all of the atmospheric activity had been positively beautiful, with flashes of light and colors so unusual that Gemma didn't even have names for them. Unfortunately, she hadn't really been able to enjoy it, because she'd had to close her eyes to avoid feeling sick. And this from a girl who loved starcoasters more than anything! While she wanted her mission to be a fast one so she could return home quickly, the thought of reattaching herself to her shooting star for the return trip was terrifying. Thank goodness for those meditation skills that Piper had shared with her; they came in very handy. By focusing on her breathing, she was able to keep calm on the trip.

Saying good-bye on the Wishworld Surveillance Deck had been quite a melancholy experience. Not only because she had always pictured Lady Stella sending her off, but because her sister had been positively teary. Tessa had hugged her so long and so hard that Gemma had had to gently push her away so she could take off. And Lady Cordial's final words to her—"always look ahead, not over your shoulder"—seemed to contradict the words she had heard in her head just before she had received her Wish Orb. Now she didn't know what to think.

Gemma had landed in a small wooded area, shielded by trees and bushes in fiery shades of yellow, orange, and red. After she folded up and carefully put away her shooting star, she pushed her way out. She realized that she was standing in the middle of a field filled with orange spheres that appeared to be growing out of the ground. It immediately brought her a sense of familiarity. A farm! A sign hanging nearby read HAPPY HALLOWEEN FROM MACDONALD'S PICK-YOUR-OWN PUMPKIN FARM. It was illustrated with an orange pumpkin (she presumed that was what it was, at least) with a scary face carved into it. A holiday that seemed to celebrate both the harvest and spooky things. How curious!

Gemma watched as families wandered about, looking at pumpkins, lifting them up, and sometimes carrying them off, but more often than not setting them back down and moving on to the next pumpkin. The chosen pumpkins were carried to a rustic-looking red building nearby. Gemma took a closer look at the structure and nearly screamed. The most enormous black spider she had ever seen was perched on the top, its colossal web covering the entire side of the building. How horrifying! Wishworld spiders were way uglier (and bigger) than their Starland counterparts, that was for sure. But then she noticed that families were walking into the building, directly underneath the horrible creature, hardly even looking up at it, and her pulse started to return to normal. Lady Cordial had warned her not to waste any time recording Wishworld observations in her Cyber Journal, but if she had, it would have been: *Mission 12, Wishworld Observation #1: Wishworld spiders are STARNORMOUS! But evidently, not dangerous. Or even noteworthy.*

Tentatively, Gemma took a step closer to the building, then another. She stopped and stared up at it. Had the spider just moved one of its eight spindly legs or was her mind playing tricks on her?

"Pretty scary, huh?" said a voice right behind her.

Gemma jumped. She whirled around to find two girls standing there, smiling at her. The taller one had short straight brown hair and green eyes that sparkled. The shorter girl had wavy shoulder-length blond hair and warm brown eyes. Gemma's hands flew to her ears as she felt a tingling sensation.

"Ooh, nice earrings," said the blond girl. "How do they glow like that?"

Is one of these girls my Wisher? Gemma wondered. *Could it possibly be that easy?* She hoped the answers were yes and yes.

"That spider has been in my family for generations," said the brown-haired girl. "As a matter of fact, my grandpa MacDonald used to hang it up with *his* grandfather, Angus. He was my"—she thought for a moment—"great-great grandfather."

"So you're a MacDonald?" Gemma asked, pointing to the sign.

"I'm Zoe," said the girl. "Welcome to MacDonald's farm."

"E-i-e-i-o," said the blond girl, thoroughly confusing Gemma.

"Don't you ever get tired of that joke, Cici?" Zoe asked, rolling her eyes. Gemma sensed a tinge of annoyance in her voice and wondered if Cici was insulted.

But Cici just laughed. "Nope," she said. Then she leaned in to look more closely at Gemma. "You didn't really think that spider was real, did you?" she asked.

"Oh, my st—I mean, goodness, of course not!" said Gemma. "How silly! I mean, of course it's fake!"

"So are you new in town or something?" Zoe asked. "I haven't seen you around at school."

"I am new and my name is Gemma," she said truthfully. "I just arrived. It was a long journey and it was quite eventful! What a ride it was. All the way from . . ." She paused. All the way from where? *Stop talking, Gemma,* she told herself. *Just stop talking!*

Luckily, Cici jumped in. "Well, you came at the right time!" she said. "We celebrate Halloween big around here. I hope you have a costume!"

Gemma vaguely recalled learning about Halloween in Wishworld Relations class, but the details were fuzzy. Maybe she had forgotten to put her headphones on that night and hadn't absorbed that day's lesson. She searched her brain for details. Was that the holiday when Wishlings ate a large roasted fowl with their family? Or the one when they pinched fellow Wishlings if they weren't wearing the color green, and had a big parade?

Suddenly, Cici's eyes widened. "Don't look now!" she said in a loud whisper. "But Maddie and Kaila are headed our way!"

Zoe looks both excited and nervous. "Do I look okay?" she asked.

"Are you afraid of heights?" Cici asked.

Zoe looks confused for a moment. "No," she answered. "What does that have to do with anyth—"

"Well, your zipper is."

Zoe seemed down in a panic, then realized she was wearing a skirt. "Cici, you nearly gave me a heart attack," she said.

"Sorry," said Cici. "I thought it was funny."

"It wasn't," said Zoe icily. Then she put a huge fake-looking smile on her face as the two girls stepped up to them. They looked almost identical, with long, straight light brown hair, off-the-shoulder oversized sweaters, and short shorts over patterned tights and tall boots. They both wore knit hats. Gemma looked from one to the other. Were they wearing some sort of uniform?

"Hi, Maddie. Hi, Kaila," said Zoe in a rush. "You know Cici, of course. And this is Gemma. She just moved here."

"Hi, Gemma," said one of the girls, her eyes flickering over Gemma from head to toe, taking in her ripped jeans, flannel shirt, and beat-up ankle boots. Gemma must have passed muster, because she nodded at her. "Cool earrings. So where are you from?"

Gemma opened her mouth. "Um, from . . . well, it's actually quite far away. . . ." Her voice trailed off.

The girl quickly lost interest and turned back to Zoe.

Gemma stared at the girls. Now which one was which? They were hard to tell apart. She wondered if she should ask them, but then she decided to keep her mouth shut. She was realizing that speaking as little as possible on Wishworld was the best way to go. It was a struggle and perhaps would be the biggest challenge of her mission.

"Is it always so dirty here?" asked one of the girls, grimacing at her dusty boots.

"Well, it *is* a farm," Cici offered. "Dirt is kind of necessary."

The girls glanced at Cici, then returned their attention to Zoe. "So my mom sent us here to get a pumpkin. Can you help us?"

Zoe smiled. "Sure," she said. She turned to Gemma and Cici. "Be back in a couple of minutes."

Cici sighed as she watched them walk off. "Zoe

really wants us to be friends with Maddie and Kaila. I guess it's okay. They're super popular and really into clothes and stuff. But they seem fake to me." She looked at Gemma. "Hey, what happened to your earrings?" she said disappointedly. "They're not glowing anymore."

What happened is that I just got confirmation that Zoe is my Wisher! Gemma thought triumphantly. She leaned in close to Cici. "So would you say that Zoe really wishes to be friends with those girls?"

Cici nodded. "Yeah. She talks about it all the time."

"Hmmm," said Gemma. She was confused. Friendship seemed like a positive wish. Based on Cici's comment about them seeming fake, Gemma wondered if they'd make good friends for Zoe. Perhaps they had positive attributes that she had not yet seen.

"Are they really fun or nice?" she asked. "Or smart, or maybe interesting? Do you like them?"

Cici shifted as if she was uncomfortable. "Well . . . they are very popular," she said slowly. "And fashionable, for sure. Nice?" She paused. "I wouldn't go that far. But if that's what Zoe wants, I'm fine with it."

"You're a good friend to Zoe," said Gemma.

Cici's smile lit up her whole face. "She's my best friend," she said. "Ever since the first day of preschool."

All right, then, thought Gemma. It seemed way too easy, but she had been counting on a quick mission, so this was working out just right.

"Listen, it's time for me to leave for my brother's basketball game tonight," said Cici. "Maybe I'll see you tomorrow at the carnival."

"Carnival?" said Gemma.

"Oh, that's right, you're new. There's this awesome carnival with rides and food and games. Then there's a parade and costume judging," explained Cici excitedly. "Zoe and I almost always win a prize. We come up with the best costumes! One year we were bacon and eggs and another year we were Bert and Ernie. And we make them all by ourselves."

"We don't have to decorate for it, do we?" Gemma asked warily, afraid she was going to be put on another committee.

"Oh, no!" Cici laughed. "We just show up and have fun." She turned to leave. "So, see you tomorrow?" she asked.

"You can count on it," said Gemma. "I wouldn't miss it for the worlds—I mean, world."

After Cici left, Gemma leaned against the wall of the barn and squinted down at her Star-Zap. *Starf!* There was only twenty-four hours left on the Countdown Clock! She knew that was one Wishworld day. Lady Cordial had said it should be a quick mission, but this was cutting it close!

She spotted Zoe and the two girls across the field, deep in conversation. *Is there that much to say about pumpkins?* she wondered. She headed toward them. As she got closer she caught a snippet of the conversation. She heard "It'll be fun" and "You'll look great," then "It's up to you. No pressure."

"So see you tonight," one of the girls said. She nodded at Gemma. "You can bring her if you want." The girls took off, carrying a medium-sized pumpkin between them.

"See you later!" called Zoe, waving after them. They didn't turn around. "Thanks for shopping at MacDonald Farms!" Then she slapped her forehead with her palm. "That was so lame. Ugh! Why did I say that?"

"So you want to be friends with those girls?" Gemma asked. It was pretty clear, but with time of the essence, she wanted confirmation from her Wisher herself.

"More than anything," said Zoe. "And they asked me to hang out with them tonight. I'm totally nervous. You'll come, right?"

"No need to be nervous," said Gemma. "I'll help you." A shiver ran down her spine so suddenly that it made the tiny hairs on her arms stand up. She guessed that was the confirmation she was looking for.

Her Wish Mission was under way.

CHAPTER
7

Zoe flipped through the pages of a glossy magazine. "It looks good. Now, you're sure this is cool?"

"I'm sure," said Gemma confidently. She had spent
the afternoon wandering around town, making observations and collecting information she thought would help
her Wisher on her quest to win over these new friends.
They were obviously very into fashion, so she looked
in all the store windows until she found a place selling
clothes that looked trendy and cool. Luckily, the owner
was bored and just as chatty as Gemma. She showed her
the latest Wishworld trends and even gave her an extra
copy she had of the cool new fashion magazine. "It's the
first issue," she said. "This will really impress the little

fashionistas!" Gemma left with a new admiration for Wishworld fashion. While it was certainly not as sparkly as Starland fashion, it was pretty startacular in its own way.

Zoe tucked the thick magazine into her backpack and the two girls wandered down the street side by side. The sun was beginning to set and the streetlamps started to turn on. Gemma had noticed that many of the stores were decorated with what she assumed were Halloween decorations—green-faced ladies with pointy hats, black winged creatures that looked a lot like bitbats, white-sheeted figures with dark holes for eyes. Gemma pointed to a pumpkin carved with a spooky face, flickering light shining through its eyes, nose, and mouth. "Spooky!" she said.

"They should know better than to leave that out on Mischief Night!" said Zoe, shaking her head.

"I thought it was Halloween," said Gemma, feeling thoroughly confused.

"Around here the night before Halloween is called Mischief Night," Zoe explained. "Kids go around smashing pumpkins, egging cars, TP'ing houses . . . you know."

Of course Gemma didn't know, but she nodded as if this all made perfect sense.

"My family hates Mischief Night," said Zoe. "One year someone took the giant spider off the roof and covered it with shaving cream. It took forever to wash it off. I'm lucky my parents let me out tonight."

"So was Cici invited to come tonight, too?" Gemma asked.

A cloud passed over Zoe's face. She shoved her hands into her jacket pockets and concentrated on a crack in the sidewalk. "No, she wasn't invited. Luckily, she had her brother's basketball game tonight, so she won't know."

"So Maddie and Kaila don't want to be friends with both of you," Gemma said slowly. She had an uneasy feeling and again wondered what made this wish—one that involved befriending not-so-nice girls and leaving out a real friend—a good one.

Zoe's voice sounded a little strangled as she spoke. "It's just really hard. Cici is fun and loyal and smart, but she's just not . . ." Zoe had a pained look on her face. "She's just not very cool."

"Cool is important?" asked Gemma.

"If you want to be popular, it is," Zoe said with a sigh. "I mean, look at Maddie and Kaila."

"What makes them so popular?" Gemma wanted to know.

"Well, they wear nice clothes, and they listen to the coolest music, and all the kids like them, and they get invited to all the parties, and everyone copies what they do," Zoe said in a rush. "I'm just . . . I'm just . . . tired of being boring. I really think I'd like that, too. And they seem to want to be my friends. So this is my chance. I can still be friends with Cici. We just won't be able to spend all our time together. She'll understand. It's no big deal."

Gemma shook her head. Was Zoe trying to convince Gemma—or herself?

Zoe stiffened. "Here they come," she whispered harshly. "Act natural." That made Gemma giggle a bit. How else was she supposed to act? The two girls crossed the street and stepped up to them, in two brand-new matching outfits—short dresses with cropped jackets and ankle boots.

Gemma wondered if Zoe was going to have to buy a brand-new wardrobe to hang out with these girls.

"Hi!" Gemma said. "Aren't you cold?" she asked, noticing their bare legs.

Maddie (Gemma thought it was Maddie, anyway) barked out a laugh. "Who cares, as long as we look great?"

Gemma nodded politely. "Of course," she said.

Zoe was rooting around in her backpack frantically. She pulled out a half-eaten bag of pretzels, three tubes of something called ChapStick, and, finally, the magazine.

"What do you have there?" Kaila asked curiously, pointing to the magazine Zoe was holding.

"The newest fashion magazine!" Zoe said proudly. "*Chic*!" But she pronounced it like *chick*. Gemma grimaced. She was pretty sure that was wrong.

The girls laughed. "Oh, Zoe, you're always so funny," Maddie said. "I've never heard of *Chic*, but it looks uh-maze-ing."

The girls flipped through the magazine. "Can we borrow this?" Kaila asked.

"Sure!" said Zoe happily. Gemma smiled. Her plan was working.

Gemma was all set for a fun time with the three girls. What would they do? She was excited to find out the fun things that Wishling kids—especially cool, popular ones—did for fun. But the evening was a bit of a disappointment. They wandered around, meeting up with groups of kids at different places around town. They went to the arcade, but they didn't play games. They went to the ice cream parlor, but they didn't order anything, even though the ice cream looked amazingly delicious. They waited outside the movie theater, but they never went inside. Then they headed to a long building called Lucky Lanes.

"Ooh! Are we bowling?" Zoe asked excitedly. "Cici and—I mean, I love to bowl!"

Maddie laughed. "Zoe, you have so much to learn. Nobody actually bowls. That's for losers. We hang out." She looked sharply at Zoe. "I mean, like I'm going to wear a pair of stinky bowling shoes with this outfit? Uh-uh."

Zoe laughed. It sounded forced to Gemma. Zoe nodded. "I was just kidding. Of course." She glanced at Gemma. "Is something wrong?" she said. "You look pale."

Gemma was feeling a bit weak. She excused herself and left to find the bathroom. It was empty, so Gemma quickly recited her Mirror Mantra, "Make up your mind to blaze like a comet!" she said, and she was instantly rewarded with the sight of herself in all her sparkly orange glory. She smiled at her bright orange hair, her glittering skin. She felt like herself again! She had renewed energy and a sense of purpose. She was going to grant this wish if it was the last thing she did. She just had to get past her negative feelings and help make this wish come true.

She pushed open the door and strode back out into

the bowling alley, its air filled with bouncy music and the crashing sound of large round objects knocking into pins.

She found Zoe leaning over, stuffing something into her backpack. Gemma was about to ask what it was when Maddie and Kaila rushed up, giggling excitedly. "Come on!" they said. "Now the fun is going to start. Eddie McNoonan has dozens of eggs and tons of shaving cream. Mischief Night has begun!"

Zoe's face fell. "Um . . . I . . ."

"Sorry, guys," said Gemma quickly. "But I have to get home and I promised my mom I would walk home with Zoe."

"Fine," said Maddie. She leaned in close to Zoe. "Now don't forget to meet us at the parade tomorrow."

"I won't," said Zoe. "Have fun!"

But one thing confused Gemma. Why had Maddie's message sounded more like a threat than a reminder?

CHAPTER
8

Gemma sat on the bed watching Zoe and Cici as they stood in front of the full-length mirror in Zoe's bedroom, giggling. Gemma couldn't help laughing, too. Cici was wearing a poorly fitting dress in a cheap, shiny material with a garish print. The hem of a white slip stuck out underneath the skirt. On her legs were black tights with runs in them, and she wore what Gemma could describe only as sensible lace-up shoes. She wore a pair of dark eyeglasses that were fastened together across the bridge with tape. Her hair was done up in a hugely unflattering three-ponytail style. Zoe wore slicked-back hair, a similar pair of taped-up glasses, a garish plaid shirt in shades of brown and blue, a clashing red-and-yellow plaid bow tie, and pants that were pulled up practically to her armpits, explosing her white socks. Black lace-up shoes completed her ensemble.

"You are both totally hideous!" said Gemma.

"Thank you!" they replied in unison.

"But . . . um . . . what are you supposed to be?" Gemma asked.

"Why, we're nerds, of course!" Zoe answered, still admiring her reflection.

The two girls turned and looked at Gemma. "Where's your costume?" Cici asked. "Go put it on!"

Gemma grabbed her backpack (which presumably held her nonexistent costume), walked into the bathroom, and closed the door. What should she be? The only costumes that came to her were Starlandian ones—a glion, a star ball player, a bunch of ozziefruit. Not exactly appropriate for Wishworld. She wondered if she could even access costumes on the Wishworld Outfit Selector.

"Hurry up!" called Zoe. "It's time to go to the carnival!" Gemma had to think fast. Then she smiled. She knew exactly what to do. She looked into the mirror and did her thing.

"Holy guacamole!" Zoe said as Gemma walked into the room. "You look amazing, Gemma!"

Cici stared. "Wow," she simply said.

The costume that Gemma had chosen to wear was

actually not a costume at all. It was Gemma's real sparkly Starlandian appearance. It made perfect sense—since she was there on a holiday when Wishlings changed their looks, she could revert to her true appearance. It was liberating and fun.

"How in the world did you manage to get ready so quickly?" Zoe asked, marveling at Gemma's sparkly skin and glittery hair.

And Gemma simply answered, "Practice."

Gemma discovered that she was totally in love with Halloween. Not only was the predominant color her favorite, but it was just so carefree and jolly and fun. Everyone was dressed up—babies in strollers, big kids, little kids, and even some adults. One man was dressed like a chef, and he held a pot with a little baby sitting inside it dressed up as a bright red creature with big claws. Some people simply wore white sheets with eyeholes cut out. There were monsters, and ladies with green faces and pointy hats. Even some pets were dressed up. Everyone was smiling and having fun.

As the girls stood in line for a deliciously airy and sweet Wishworld delicacy called cotton candy, Maddie and Kaila showed up. They were wearing high heels, tons of makeup, slinky-looking gold dresses, fake fur coats, large sunglasses, and flowing wigs—one blond, one brunette. Gemma almost didn't recognize them under all the makeup.

"Wow," said Gemma, amazed by their fancy costumes. "What are you two dressed up as?"

Kaila tossed her head a little too hard, and her wig slipped to the side, covering half her face. "We're supermodels, of course," she said, yanking her hair back into place.

Maddie leaned forward and touched Gemma's arm, surprised that no glitter came off on her hand. "Where did you get that body glitter?" she asked. "It's awesome."

"Um . . . I brought it from home," Gemma answered.

"And look at you two!" Maddie said to Zoe and Cici. "Very funny!"

Zoe didn't answer, but Cici thanked her.

"See you later," Maddie said, looking directly at Zoe, who nodded, then looked away.

Gemma half expected the wish energy to pour off Zoe right then and there. The girls were obviously accepting her as a friend. And wasn't that just what she wanted? As much as Gemma was enjoying Halloween, it was time for her to return to Starland.

After Gemma, Zoe, and Cici went on rides (pretty tame compared to those on Starland), played several games of chance (Gemma won a large stuffed white-horned galliope, which she immediately gave to a little kid), and ate every treat there was to try (cotton candy was the winner, followed closely by something called fried dough), it was time for the parade.

The girls lined up with all the other costumed kids. Music began to play, and slowly, everyone began to march. It was a procession down the main street of the town, ending when they reached the town square, where a stage was set up for the costume judging. People lined the streets to cheer on the costumed marchers, who waved like they were starlebrities. When Gemma saw people pointing and cheering just for her, being herself, she felt very proud. For a second she thought she saw a familiar face in the crowd, but she figured she was just feeling homesick.

When they reached the end of the parade route, she had somehow gotten separated from Cici and Zoe in the mob of kids. She heard someone calling her name and turned around with a smile, expecting it to be one of the "nerds." To her surprise, Gemma saw Leona pushing through the crowd toward her.

"Oh, my stars!" Leona said when she reached Gemma's side. "How perfect! You can be your Starlandian self today because everyone is in costume! What a great idea!"

Gemma nodded proudly. Then she frowned. "Why are you here, Leona?" she asked a little testily. "I've got everything under control."

"Then I guess I'm just here for support," said Leona with a shrug.

"So what's been going on back home?" Gemma asked eagerly. "Did you find Lady Stella?"

Leona shook her head. "They're still looking. We went to Lady Cordial for help, but she was useless."

"So why did they send you?" Gemma asked again. "You've already been a helper on a mission. I was expecting Tessa, actually." If someone had to come help her on Wishworld, she would have liked it to be her big sister. It would have been startastic for Tessa to see her collecting her wish energy.

"It's kind of weird," said Leona. "The rest of the Star Darlings were concentrating on finding Lady Stella, but Tessa and I started getting worried about you. We hadn't heard anything from Lady Cordial, but we didn't trust her to be paying attention to your orb. So we decided that Tessa would make the trip to see how things were going. We brought Astra along, too, and headed to the Wishworld Surveillance Deck. Astra had just lassoed the star, and we were struggling to hold on to it so Tessa could get strapped in, when all of a sudden something told me that I needed to go instead. It was like a voice in my head. It said, 'It's your turn, Leona. Go and help Gemma!' So, um, I kind of pushed Tessa out of the way and strapped myself in. She was pretty mad, as you can imagine. She was yelling and shaking her fist at me as I took off!"

Gemma smiled a little, imagining her irate sister.

"So how much time is left on the Countdown Clock?" asked Leona.

"A half starhour," said Gemma anxiously. She took a deep breath. "But I have a feeling that the wish is going to come true when the girls are onstage during the costume judging." She smiled. "I'm pretty sure they are going to win a prize for best costume, and that's what will end up making Zoe part of the popular crowd."

"Your Wisher's wish is to become popular?" Leona asked. "That's a good wish?"

Gemma shrugged. "I know. It seems weird. But she's really a nice person, so I guess it's somehow got to be a good wish."

"Talk about taking it down to the starwire," said

Leona with a whistle. "Very dramatic. So what are they dressed as?"

"Nerds," said Gemma.

Leona looked at her uncomprehendingly.

"From what I can tell, nerds are unfashionable-looking Wishlings," Gemma explained. "Um, like they wear ugly clothes and broken accessories."

Leona made a face. "So why do Wishlings like to dress up as them?" she asked.

"Your guess is as good as mine," said Gemma.

The Star Darlings watched as Wishlings lined up, were introduced by the announcer, walked across the stage, and stood in front of the table of judges, who scored them. A group of Wishlings—a girl in a blue-and-white checked dress and sparkly red shoes (that would have fit right in on Starland); a woman with a green face and a pointy hat; a silver man with a pointy hat; a large glion; and a man who seemed to be made of straw in raggedy clothing—were apparently from a movie called something like *The Blizzard of Frogs*. A bunch of girls with bodysuits that matched their skin tones, jewels in their belly buttons, and big brightly colored wigs were something called trolls. The crowd loved them all.

Gemma grabbed Leona's hand and squeezed it as she

spotted Cici in the wings. "This is it," she said. "They're about to come onstage."

Gemma stood on her toes so she could get an unobstructed view of the wish coming true. She had to remind herself to breathe; she was hardly able to contain her excitement.

Cici walked onstage, followed by Zoe. Gemma took one look and gasped. Something was wrong. Very wrong.

CHAPTER 9

Leona shook her head. "I don't get it," she said. Cici was still in her nerd outfit, dangling slip and all. But Zoe had changed. She was in a costume that looked remarkably similar to the ones Maddie and Kaila had been wearing earlier. Makeup. Wig. Fancy shiny dress. Heels. The announcer called them onstage. Cici walked to the middle of the stage, then stopped short. Zoe bumped into her. The two girls began arguing.

Gemma clutched Leona's arm. "I don't like this one bit," she said.

"Whenever you're ready, girls," said the announcer.

Zoe took a few wobbly steps forward. She turned back and gestured for Cici to follow. Cici shook her head. Zoe motioned again, and then finally, reluctantly, Cici walked forward and stood next to Zoe.

Even the announcer looked confused. "And what are you two dressed as?" he asked.

Zoe hesitated for a moment.

"They're chic and the geek!" a voice called out from the audience. Gemma craned her neck to see Maddie and Kaila standing in the front row. They were laughing hysterically. The crowd laughed, too. "I'll say!" someone yelled.

"Chic and the geek?" said the announcer.

Zoe looked awkward and uncertain. Cici was clearly miserable.

"My Wisher just turned her wish into something really bad," Gemma whispered. "And I helped her do it. This is terrible."

Cici stood for a moment as the laughter washed over her. Then she bolted off the stage.

Leona and Gemma watched in horror as an arc of dark swirling colors invisible to everyone but them began to ooze from Zoe and sluggishly creep toward Gemma. She wanted to flee. But she was frozen in place as the horrible energy was sucked into her Wish Pendant. She suddenly felt very heavy and dull, as if she could barely stand.

Leona turned toward Gemma, her eyes wide. "That can't be good," she said. It was the understatement of the staryear.

"Oh, my stars," said Gemma. "What have I done?"

Leona found Gemma a bench to sit on. Gemma put her head between her legs and breathed deeply.

★

"We have to fix this," said Leona. "There must be a way." She paused. "Have you discovered what your special talent is?" she asked.

"No," said Gemma, lifting her head.

"Think, Gemma, think," said Leona. "We need to reverse this somehow."

Gemma buried her face in her hands. This was the twelfth and final mission. The last chance to collect enough wish energy to save Starland. And she had ruined things for everyone.

"I only collected bad energy!" she cried. "How bad is this for Starland?"

"It's pretty bad," said Leona. "While you were away, the wish energy scientists released some more information. It turns out that if the wish energy balance on Starland is shifted toward the negative, there won't be energy to do anything. No Starcars, no Star-Zaps, no lights. But that's not the worst of it. The worst thing is that as the negative overtakes the positive, everyone on Starland will lose their joy and become sad and mean. We won't be able to grant wishes anymore, so the Wishers will lose their joy, too."

Gemma shivered. "Maybe I'll just have to stay here. Keep the negative energy here with me."

"Maybe," said Leona. "But I'm not even sure it works that way."

Gemma thought about the possibility of never seeing her parents again and felt like her heart would break. She supposed she'd possibly be able to see her sister and the other Star Darlings if there continued to be missions. That was the one ray of starshine in a bleak future.

"There you are!" someone shouted. "You have to help me!"

Gemma lifted her head again. Zoe rushed up to them, her wig askew.

"What was I thinking?" she cried. "I made a huge mistake. I got so caught up in impressing Maddie and Kaila that I ruined the most important friendship I've ever had."

She sank down onto a nearby bench and thrust her hands into her luxurious blond wig. "Can you help me?

Please?" Zoe looked quizzically at Leona and back to Gemma.

"This is my friend Leona," Gemma hurriedly explained. "We really want to help you," she added fervently.

"Hi," said Leona. "You really were a bad friend to Cici."

Zoe couldn't make eye contact with either of them. "I know," she whispered.

"What happened to your new friends?" asked Leona.

"It didn't last too long," said Zoe with a wry smirk. "Right afterwards, I just felt awful about what I had done. Then Maddie and Kaila came over with all their friends and they started laughing at Cici and saying that she really was a nerd, and I thought to myself, 'Oh, yeah? Well, I am, too! And we nerds have way more fun than people like you, who just stand around making fun of people. You're so afraid of looking stupid that you never do anything!' And then I realized everyone was staring at me, because I had said it out loud."

Leona sat next to Zoe and grabbed her hands. "You have to realize that you made a selfish wish followed by a bad choice. And here's the thing—our wishes and our choices tell the world who we really are. So you've got to choose and wish wisely."

Zoe sniffed. "I know that now," she said. "And I'll never forget it. I learned it the hardest way of all."

She ripped the wig off her head and threw it to the ground.

Gemma blew out her breath sharply. "Poor you. Poor us."

Leona pulled Gemma to the side. She put her hand to her forehead. "Poor Cici," she said, pointing to the girl, who was standing alone in the crowd. Cici's exaggerated nerd costume made her look even sadder. Leona laughed bitterly. "She looks like she just lost her best friend."

"Thanks to me," said Gemma, her voice despondent. A ruined friendship, a missed chance to collect positive energy, and a Wish Pendant full of negative wish energy. Could things be any worse? This was a very grim future, indeed.

Suddenly, she remembered the words she had heard in the hallway back on Starland: *While looking to the future, you must not forget the past.* She said the words out loud, softly, and a jolt of energy went through her. She closed her eyes and concentrated on the past.

When she opened her eyes, she watched in disbelief as Leona put her hand to her forehead again. "Poor Cici," she said again, pointing to the girl. She laughed bitterly. "She looks like she just lost her best friend." Again.

Gemma grinned.

Leona gave Gemma a funny look as a realization hit. "Wait a minute! Did you just . . . ?"

"I did!" Gemma crowed. "My talent must be to turn back time! Oh, my stars, we just might be able to fix this after all!"

This time Gemma managed not to get separated from Zoe and Cici after the parade. She followed Zoe as she walked to the park bench where she had stashed her backpack. Stuffed inside was the supermodel costume that Gemma now knew Maddie and Kaila had handed her in the bowling alley the night before. Gemma grabbed the bag from Zoe's hand. "Don't do it," she said. "Embrace the nerd!"

Zoe looked as though she'd been caught red-handed. "But how did you . . . ?"

Gemma smiled. "Don't worry about it. Just know that you're better than this."

"But . . ." Zoe looked over at Maddie and Kaila, who stood in front of the stage with a group of friends, laughing and joking.

"You have a choice to make," said Gemma. "True friendship or popularity."

"Leave me alone!" said Zoe. She slung the bag over her shoulder and stalked off.

Gemma chewed her lip as she watched her disappear into the crowd. Which choice would Zoe make?

"So what happened?" asked Leona when Gemma joined her.

"I don't know," said Gemma. "I guess we'll know soon enough."

So Gemma and Leona watched as Cici walked onstage alone. "And what is your costume?" the announcer asked.

Cici blinked at him. "I'm waiting for a friend," she said. "If you could just give me one more minute, I'm sure that she'll be here."

Just then there was a commotion that sounded like someone pushing her way toward the stage. Gemma held her breath as she waited for the person to appear. It was Zoe.

The announcer asked, once again, "And what is your costume?"

And Zoe said, "We're nerds. Me and my best friend, Cici, are nerds."

CHAPTER
10

Gemma felt as light as air. It didn't hurt that she was zipping through the heavens—not a meteorite in sight—on her way back to Starland. She was bringing back positive wish energy in her Wish Pendant. But she had collected an awful lot of negative wish energy, too. Would the positive energy win out over the negative? She didn't know. Despite her worry, she smiled as she recalled how Maddie and Kaila had thrown up their hands in disgust when Zoe showed up onstage in her nerd outfit, signaling to them that she had made a choice—true friendship over popularity. That had felt awfully good.

Gemma landed right behind the dorms and headed inside. The halls were completely empty and her footfalls echoed. Through a window she saw a fourth-year Starling Academy student passing by. She ran to the door, pushed it open, and followed her. "Hey! Where is everyone?" she called.

"Where have you been?" asked the girl. "It's Starshine Day! Everyone is in the Star Quad. It's almost time for the Battle of the Bands. You don't want to miss that!"

It was already Starshine Day! Gemma's stomach did a flip. Talk about cutting it close. She couldn't wait to tell Lady Cordial that it looked like her premonition just might be correct. That everything might turn out exactly the way it was supposed to. That her mission would turn the tide for Starland and return it to the way it was meant to be.

Lady Cordial had predicted that this would happen just in time for Starshine Day. And here it was, really happening.

Gemma took a deep breath, smoothed back her hair, and headed to the Star Quad.

When Gemma reached the quad, she could see the briteflower garlands draped from pillar to pillar, shining beautifully, and she felt a little swell of pride in her handiwork. There was a glimmerbounce house, bumper Starcars, even a mini starcoaster. The smell of grilled garble greens filled the air, and Starlings were walking around, laughing and chatting. It was as if everyone had forgotten about the shortage and they were just allowing themselves to relax and enjoy the day. And maybe that was the point.

Gemma heard Lady Cordial's voice over the loudspeaker. "Introducing S-s-s-starlight S-s-s-starbright, the first contestant in S-s-s-starling Academy's Battle of the Bands!" she announced. The crowd roared.

The quad was packed with Starlings, so Gemma took the long way around, past the hedge maze. As she passed the entrance to the hedge maze, she heard a sound. *Psst! Psst!*

Whoa! The next thing she knew, someone had grabbed her arm and she was being yanked backward into the maze. She spun around. "What in the stars!" she exclaimed. Vega stood there, looking grim.

"What's going on? Did you find Lady Stella yet?" Gemma asked.

But Vega just spun on her heel and started walking

quickly into the maze. Not wanting to be left behind, Gemma raced after her. "Vega! Say something! What in the stars in going on?"

"Just follow me," Vega hissed. In only a couple of turns, they were in the center of the maze. It would have taken Gemma forever if she had been by herself.

There, facing her, were all the Star Darlings, including Leona. Then they all took a step forward. And there, in all her regal beauty, was Lady Stella.

Without a word, Gemma ran toward her, throwing her arms around the headmistress. "Oh, Lady Stella, Lady Stella." It was all she could say.

The headmistress stroked Gemma's hair gently. "Oh, Gemma, I hope your mission wasn't too overwhelming," she said. "I heard it was a difficult one."

Gemma felt like she might burst into tears if she said a word. She took a step backward. She noticed that another adult stood nearby, her arms around Sage. They looked so much alike, right down to their pointy elfin chins. "Indirra!" said Gemma.

Indirra smiled gently. "It's so good to be here," she said.

"Tell her the story!" said Sage eagerly. "But quickly! We're due onstage soon, so there isn't much time!"

"Cassie, you figured it out. You tell the story," said Lady Stella.

Cassie smiled at Lady Stella gratefully. "Well, Sage and I were really getting worried. Neither Lady Stella nor Indirra was anywhere to be found. We called all the Star Darlings together but no one had any idea what to do, and everyone was getting really frustrated. Then Itty started singing. I scooped her up and tried shushing her, but she just wouldn't stop. I was about to put her in the closet when I stopped and listened to the words. She was singing the 'Song of Secrets'! And the song told the story of two beautiful women who were trapped in a cave at the base of the Crystal Mountains against their will! We were hoping against hope that it was Lady Stella and Indirra. But we weren't sure. Then we realized that the song rhymed 'star-protection suits' with 'forbidden fruits' and 'shovel' with 'on the double.' We grabbed those things and took off immediately, a little scared at what we might find."

Cassie paused to take a breath and Adora took up the story next. "When we got to the foothills of the mountains, we found a cave entrance blocked off by the hugest pile of the most beautiful crystal shards. But as soon as we got close, we all started bickering and feeling extremely tired and angry. They were clearly infused with negative energy! So we put on the suits and started digging. We dug and dug, and after what felt like forever, we finally reached the entrance. And there stood Lady Stella and Indirra!"

Lady Stella smiled at the girls. "You have no idea how happy we were to see you. I explained that when I was confronted"—here she placed a hand on Cassie's shoulder reassuringly—"I realized that someone had to be framing me. I panicked and disappeared in a flash and headed to the Crystal Caves. I contacted Indirra to meet me there so we could come up with a plan together. But as soon as we stepped inside the cave, disaster struck. There was a huge avalanche and we were trapped. My Star-Zap had gotten crushed in the avalanche and Indirra's wouldn't work. The negative energy was making us weaker and weaker. We were beginning to despair of ever escaping. Then, as we were drifting off to sleep one night, we heard the familiar 'Song of Comfort.' That's when we realized we shared the cave with a gaggle of glowfurs! Quickly we made up a song and taught it to them, knowing they would pass it on to every other glowfur they met, as is their tradition. I just hoped it would get to Itty quickly."

Gemma had to interrupt. "So you knew about Cassie's secret pet?"

Lady Stella just gave her a look and Gemma blushed. Of course the headmistress had known. She knew everything about her students. That was the kind of headmistress she was.

Sage's mother spoke next. "And then we waited. And then the Star Darlings came!"

"And we started talking and I discovered that my mom has known Lady Stella for a long time. She used to take me to campus when I was little, to hone my wish energy manipulation skills!" Sage said.

"They were off the charts," Indirra said proudly. "Even when she was a wee Starling."

"And that's why Mojo liked me so much!" Sage said. "He must have somehow remembered me from long ago!"

Leona stepped forward. "But why didn't you tell us you were working together? That we were the twelve Star-Charmed Starlings?" she asked.

"We didn't want to overwhelm you," explained Lady Stella. "We thought the pressure would be too much. We realize now we should have told you right away the true nature of your missions. I can promise you this, Star Darlings: there will be no more secrets going forward."

"We thought that once the twelfth Star Darling went on her mission the shortage could possibly be reversed," Indirra said. "And now you have returned, Gemma. Soon we will discover if the theory is true."

Lady Stella reached into her pocket and pulled out a

small solar-metal instrument. "This is the Wish Energy Meter. Right now it is exactly in the middle, right between positive energy and negative energy. Your mission should determine which way it will tilt."

"So, Gemma, how was your mission?" Indirra asked eagerly.

Gemma looked down at the ground. "It was terrible. Something went wrong and I collected negative wish energy."

Everyone gasped.

"But then she turned it around and collected positive energy, too!" Leona hastily offered.

Though Lady Stella looked calm, Gemma could tell she was worried. Very worried. "We'll see how things go. Stars crossed, my Starlings. Stars crossed."

Leona looked down at her Star-Zap. "Oh, *starf,* Lady Cordial is freaking out. The Star Darlings are up next!"

"Everyone, stay calm," Lady Stella commanded. She pulled her hood up over her head. Indirra did the same. "The saboteur could be out there," Lady Stella said. "We can't take any chances. We need to get that orb!"

A shiver ran down Gemma's spine. The twelfth orb. The final mission.

Had she succeeded—or had she failed?

CHAPTER
11

The Star Darlings stood in the wings—five ready to perform, seven there for emotional support—waiting nervously as Vivica's band finished its set. Leona had a grim look on her face, and Gemma wondered if it had the tiniest bit to do with the fact that the band actually sounded pretty good. A huge roar went up when they were done. The crowd apparently loved Vivica and the Visionaries.

When the crowd quieted down, Lady Cordial began to speak. "And now, introducing our final contestants— S-s-s-scarlet on drums, S-s-s-sage on lead guitar, Libby on keytar, Vega on bass guitar, and Leona on lead vocals. S-s-s-starlings, I introduce you to the S-s-s-star Darlings!"

The girls ran out to polite applause.

Astra peeked out at the crowd and gasped. "Oh, my stars! Leebeau is here! I don't think he has any idea what he is getting himself into. Who knows how tonight will end?"

Despite her nervousness, Gemma took a peek. When her eyes fell on the boy, she could understand Astra's interest. Leebeau, with his dark skin and shock of blond hair (not to mention his excellent bone structure), was stellarly cute.

Lady Cordial stepped offstage and smiled and nodded as she walked by the girls. A shiver—of either excitement or dread; she couldn't be sure which—ran down Gemma's spine.

The band began to play. The crowd was quiet at first, but as the music grew louder and faster, they began to get into it, dancing and cheering.

Each band got to play three songs. After playing "Together" and "Star-Crossed," the Star Darlings launched into "Wish Upon a Star," which turned out to be a real crowd-pleaser. When the girls were done, they took a bow. The crowd roared.

Lady Cordial scurried back onstage, clapping her hands. "Star salutations, Star Darlings, on a job well done," she cried. She shielded her eyes with her hand as she scanned the wings. "And now I will call *all* of the Star Darlings onstage. Come on, girls, don't be shy!"

Gemma started. What was Lady Cordial doing? The Starling Academy students only knew about Star Darlings the band. She wasn't the only one who was confused: the band members stood there, still holding their instruments, looking at each other.

"Yes, all of you," said Lady Cordial. "Gemma, Adora, Astra, Cassie, Piper, Clover, and Tessa, please come join us onstage."

Not sure what else to do, the rest of the girls walked out and stood blinking in front of the crowd. Lady Cordial smiled at them. "Before we name the winner of the Battle of the Bands, I have an announcement to make. Here before you stand the *real* Star Darlings. I don't mean the band. I am talking about twelve of your peers who were secretly hand-selected as the best of the best of Starling Academy. And believe it or not, these brave girls have all secretly gone down to Wishworld on missions to collect wish energy to help stop the shortage that has befallen Starland."

There was a loud gasp as the students took in this shocking news.

Gemma glanced at her sister, who looked as puzzled as she felt. Why was Lady Cordial doing this? Tessa reached over and grabbed Gemma's hand, which made Gemma feel a tiny bit better. Gemma stared at Lady Cordial. She suddenly realized something: Lady Cordial hadn't stuttered a single syllable since she had revealed the Star Darlings. And something else was different. Was it possible that Lady Cordial looked taller than usual?

What in the stars was going on?

Lady Cordial continued. "There were twelve missions in total. The last mission was taken by Gemma, who returned just starmins ago. Thanks to her hard work, the wish energy imbalance is about to be readjusted. Gemma, will you please step forward?"

Gemma gulped, dropped Tessa's hand, and did so.

Lady Cordial next reached into her pocket and pulled out Gemma's Wish Orb, still shiny and glittery. But then she did something strange. Lady Cordial blew on the orb, and the glitter fell away, revealing that it was dark and murky.

Everyone gasped. It was a Bad Wish Orb!

So that's what happened! Gemma thought. *It was a bad wish from the beginning.* She turned to Lady Cordial again and she suddenly realized that her eyes hadn't been playing tricks on her. Lady Cordial was transforming before their very eyes from the frumpy, awkward, and unremarkable headmistress to a tall and imposing presence.

Her neat purple bun had been replaced by lank gray hair. Her plump cheeks were becoming thin and sunken. And her skin, once bright and sparkly like that of most Starlings, was now dull and ashen. But Gemma could only focus on her eyes. They glittered coldly. It was hard to look away. But she did notice that the stage was suddenly surrounded by a squadron of Bot-Bot guards, all there to protect Lady Cordial.

"I, Rancora, in the guise of silly, stuttering Lady Cordial, tricked Gemma into granting a bad wish," crowed the villainess. "And now, thanks to her, the balance has been shifted—to negative wish energy—just as I planned!"

The crowd gasped again. Someone screamed.

Lady Stella, who had been watching from a distance, took a step forward. She stared up at the woman on the stage and a wave of recognition crossed her face. "Rancora," she whispered solemnly.

Gemma's stomach lurched. She could hardly believe what she was hearing. This changed everything. Her mission hadn't been a good wish gone bad at all. It was out-and-out, no question about it, a bad wish that she had granted. The negative energy she had collected would be too strong and powerful. Her mission had been a huge mistake. She had fallen for Lady Cordial's—er, Rancora's—trick. And now everything was ruined—forever.

Gemma wanted to run far, far away, but some terrible force held her in place. She watched in horror as the bulging, blackened orb lurched toward her, closer and closer. It hovered in front of her, mere star inches from her face, and she almost couldn't breathe.

What have I done? she thought, nearly overcome with despair. But then, as if in a trance, she held out her hand. The orb settled in her outstretched palm. A lovely warm feeling ran up her arm and coursed through her. And suddenly, she realized what had happened. By turning the bad wish into a good one, she must have reversed the orb!

Before Gemma's eyes, the orb transformed from a dark, misshapen thing into a beautiful glowing sphere. It felt warm and smooth and *good*. She felt strong and powerful as she held the orb above her head in triumph. "Yes, I was tricked into granting a bad wish. But what you don't know is that I turned that Wish Orb into a Good Wish Orb, Rancora! Now watch!"

Before everyone's eyes, the orb turned into a flower—a beautiful chatterburst, a vibrantly bright orange blossom, fairly bursting with energy. The Wish Blossom swiveled around to face Gemma as she inhaled its sweet orange-vanilla scent. As she stared at its filaments, hung with glowing stardust, it suddenly opened, revealing her Power Crystal—a lustrous egg-shaped scatterite, sprinkled with stardust on its perfectly smooth surface. It settled in her hand like it belonged there.

Triumphantly, Gemma held the milky orange stone up to Rancora.

But Rancora did not look scared, taken aback, or even slightly concerned. She just looked at Gemma's Power Crystal and laughed.

CHAPTER
12

"**Silly girl,**" Rancora said mockingly. "Once a bad wish is granted, you can't negate its power entirely. I. Still. Win."

"It looks like she's right, Gemma," a voice said sadly. Indirra stepped out of the shadows, holding Lady Stella's Wish Energy Meter. The arrow had lurched toward BAD and was swinging wildly back and forth. The sky grew dark and the wind started to whip. Thunder rumbled and lightning flashed.

Rancora raised her arms to the heavens and lifted her face to the stormy sky. Her lips twisted in an evil smile. "How do you stupid Star Darlings not realize that you need *all twelve* Power Crystals to have any sort of power? You're the *twelve* Star-Charmed Starlings, after all! Without that final one, your crystals are completely useless on Starland! And I destroyed Leona's Wish Pendant! It will never absorb wish energy again!"

"*You* destroyed my pendant?" Leona shouted.

"Child's play, my dear," Rancora said mockingly. "Remember the star key chains you all took along on your trips to Wishworld? I infused them with negative wish energy in order to sabotage your missions. It worked differently, yet effectively, on each mission. And luckily for me, it caused *your* Wish Pendant to malfunction. All the things you blamed on Lady Stella happened because of me. *I* sent you the flowers. *I* created the nail polish. *I* switched Scarlet's and Ophelia's grades." She laughed. "I even hypnotized everyone with the song so they would all be happy about Starshine Day, knowing it was the perfect venue to make my announcement."

"But why?" Gemma asked.

"For power, of course," she said. "The rest of you thrive on positive energy. I thrive on the negative. By upsetting the balance, now I will rule Starland!"

"Wait!" called a voice from the back of the crowd. Lady Stella walked toward the stage, the crowd parting to let her pass. She looked exceptionally calm and regal.

"Lady Stella!" someone called out.

"Well, if it isn't our dear headmistress," said Rancora. "I see you managed to escape from your crystal cave. Well, I am glad you are here, old friend, to witness the destruction of all you hold dear!"

Thunder crashed, and lightning struck a nearby kaleidoscope tree. Gemma watched as the flowers drifted to the ground like multicolored snowflakes. *How beautiful,* she thought despite herself.

"Not so fast," said Lady Stella. She reached into her pocket and pulled out a golden orb, which floated up into the air. "I've held on to this orb in the hopes that it would someday transform."

Before everyone's disbelieving eyes, the orb floated through the air, right toward Leona.

Leona's eyes were wide. She reached into her pocket, as if in a trance. Gemma had a sudden realization. The positive energy that resulted when Leona helped her turn a bad wish into a good one must have been so strong that it repaired Leona's ruined Wish Pendant. And now her Wish Orb was glowing again. No wonder she had felt an impulse to push Tessa out of the way and join Gemma on her mission!

As Leona pulled the golden cuff out of her pocket, Rancora, realizing what was about to happen, raised her hand to the pendant dangling from her neck and, opening it, poured out a cloud of negative energy and sent it soaring toward Leona. The negative energy glanced off the orb and hit the sign that hung over the stage, which was draped in briteflowers. They immediately withered and drooped. The orb, however, continued on its path. Then, just as it was about to land in Leona's outstretched hand, Rancora shot another burst of negative energy, this time directly at Leona.

"Nooooooo!" Gemma heard herself scream.

Leona stood stock-still, unable to move. Just as the negative energy was about to hit her, a Bot-Bot lunged forward and absorbed the shot. It plummeted to the stage with a crash so loud it made Gemma wince.

"That Bot-Bot saved my life," said Leona in disbelief just as the orb settled in her hand. She held her Wish Pendant in the other. It now glowed with pure golden energy, burnt and blackened no more. The orb rapidly transformed into Leona's Wish Blossom, a golden roar, which then opened to reveal her Power Crystal, a rough-cut, yellow-gold glisten paw. Gemma instinctively reached for her Power Crystal and held it up. That was when she realized that all the other Star Darlings were doing the same thing.

Rancora shot another burst of negative energy at the

Star Darlings, but this time it was as if they were surrounded by an invisible force field. It glanced off and
dissipated.

As if they were in a trance, the Star Darlings all let
go of their Power Crystals, which floated in the air in
front of them. They joined hands. The Power Crystals
glowed so brightly that everyone in the audience had to
shield their eyes and look away. Then the crystals began
to spin, faster and faster, until they were a colorful blur.

"NO!" Rancora screamed.

Indirra was still holding the Wish Energy Meter.
The arrow swung violently back and forth until it veered
so violently to the good side that it flew right off! Then
every light in Starland went on at the same time, flood-
ing it with light once more. A wave of pure good wish
energy swept over the crowd. The air was filled with
positivity and light. The crowd cheered, overwhelmed
with joy and relief.

Everyone but Rancora, that is. With a bloodcurdling
scream of anger and despair, she opened her pendant
once more, tapped out some of the powdery substance,
blew on it, and disappeared in a puff of acrid smoke that
stung Gemma's eyes.

Gemma ran over to the spot where Rancora had
seemingly disappeared into thin air. She was really gone.

Just then Gemma heard a cry. She rushed to Sage to see her kneeling over the brave Bot-Bot who had saved Leona's life.

Sage turned when Gemma touched her shoulder. "It's Mojo," she said sadly. She turned back to his still metallic body and peered down at him. "Mojo, speak to me," Sage pleaded.

But there was no answer. His face was blank, his eyes empty. Sage began to weep bitterly, the tears coursing down her face in glittery purple streaks. "Oh, Mojo," she said. "You saved us. Please wake up!"

With a whir and a shower of sparks, the Bot-Bot sat up so quickly he bumped heads with Sage. She lost her balance and landed on her bottom.

"Why are you crying, Miss Sage?" Mojo asked worriedly. "I'm fine!"

Sage rubbed her head and laughed shakily. "Oh, Mojo," she said simply. Then she stood up and jumped into the air with joy. "We did it! We did it!" she shouted, grabbing Gemma's hand and raising it in the air.

Gemma jumped up and down with her. They had done it. They had rescued Lady Stella, turned a bad wish into a good one, saved Starland. Her sister ran over and swept her into a tight hug. Relief and happiness rushed through Gemma, leaving her shaking.

There was a roar and Gemma looked around wildly. "Gemma, look!" said Tessa, pointing to the crowd. Gemma looked down to see a sea of upturned faces calling out their names, hundreds of Starlings clapping, cheering, and pointing to a spectacular rainbow glittering in the sky. Gemma noticed the bright orange aura emanating from her body and gasped as she realized that she and her fellow Star Darlings were glowing so radiantly that together they formed the most beautiful glittering rainbow anyone had ever seen.

Lady Stella stepped forward and applauded right along with the crowd. Then she motioned for the Star Darlings to gather around her. When Gemma got closer, she was confused by the look of regret on the head-mistress's face. Smiling at them sadly, Lady Stella said, "Star apologies, my Starlings." She raised her arms in the air and the crowd silenced.

"For what?" Gemma asked, but her words were swept away by the loud whooshing wind that ripped through her hair and tore the Starshine Day decorations off the stage, scattering them into the air. Gemma shielded her face with her arm. What in the stars was going on? Tessa put her arms around Gemma and the two sisters huddled together fearfully.

But their terror turned to awe as a shooting star

streaked across the sky, exploding into multicolored blossoms that fell toward their upturned faces, close enough to touch. "Ohhhhhhhhh!" said the crowd. Suddenly, the sky was dancing with colorful beams of light. The crowd and the Star Darlings were transfixed. Gemma was filled with an amazing sense of hope and beauty and pure wondrous joy.

It ended as quickly as it had begun. The Star Darlings stood blinking at each other in confusion. The air—and the mood—felt different. Something momentous had just happened—but what exactly?

Gemma looked down at the crowd. The faces were no longer looking at them in adulation. In fact, they looked confused. Some faces even looked irritated.

"Get off the stage, you Star Ding-a-lings!" someone called out.

Gemma felt her face grow slack with shock. And then, suddenly, she laughed loud and hard. The rest of the Star Darlings joined in. Their moment in the suns had been quite fleeting!

Lady Stella shook her head, her expression sympathetic. "I'm sorry, but everyone's memories have just been erased. Starland needs your special talents to remain under wraps, at least for now. I have a strong feeling this is just the beginning of your adventures. Your time in the starlight will come, Starlings. I promise."

Lady Stella turned to the crowd. "Attention, students! Now we will crown the winners of the Battle of the Bands. Will Vivica and the Visionaries and Star Light Star Bright please join the Star Darlings onstage?"

Gemma, Tessa, Cassie, Adora, Piper, Astra, and Clover moved into the wings to watch the judging. Gemma saw Leona grab Scarlet's and Libby's hands. From the pained looks on their faces she was apparently squeezing them very tightly.

"As you know, we use the Ranker in our competitions to ensure that the judging is fair and unbiased. The Ranker uses an algorithm that measures the level of crowd reaction, difficulty of music, and creativity of lyrics to choose the winner. And the winner of this year's Battle of the Bands is . . ." Lady Stella paused and consulted the Ranker. It seemed like she was moving in slow motion. Gemma realized that she was holding her breath. A Star Darlings victory would be so sweet at that very moment.

"Vivica and the Visionaries! Star kudos, Starlings, on a job well done!"

Gemma felt her heart sink down to her sparkly

orange flats. She saw the disappointed faces of the Star Darlings band, smiling bravely. But then she brightened. So they had lost the Battle of the Bands. They had won the battle for Starland—even if they were the only ones who knew it.

The Star Darlings gathered on the stargrass, where they stood in companionable silence. They were exhausted, ebullient, a tiny bit disappointed, and a whole lot proud.

"Don't look now," Gemma whispered to Sage, "but here comes Vivica."

The girls watched as the Starling made her way to them, her aura glowing pale blue. She was clutching the holo-statue she had received in her hand and had a huge smile on her face.

"Maybe she's coming to extend the kaleidoscope tree branch to us," said Gemma optimistically. "It could be now that Lady Cordial's negative influence is over, she'll be nice."

She smiled at Vivica.

"Hey, girls," Vivica said.

"Hey, Vivica," said Sage. "Star kudos on your victory."

The rest of the Star Darlings nodded.

Leona bit her lip but managed a smile. "Yeah, you put on a good show," she said.

Vivica looked down at the ground almost bashfully. "I just came over to say one thing," she began. Then she looked up and her grin turned nasty. "Beat you good, Star Dippers," she said, then spun on her heel and marched off.

Leona's mouth fell open. "Of all the . . ." she started. "I have half a mind to . . ." Her voice trailed off and she said simply, "Starf!"

Lady Stella glided over and gave the Star Darlings a sympathetic look. "Oh, my stars," she said. "That was certainly unpleasant, wasn't it? Talk about a sore winner!" She looked at Vivica's retreating back and shook her head. "We had better keep an eye on that girl. She seems like trouble."

Epilogue

A short time later, the Star Darlings stood on their own private section of the Wishworld Surveillance Deck. Lady Stella had brought them there for a confidential chat.

She smiled at them tenderly. "I want to tell you star salutations once more for saving Starland. You faced many challenges from a formidable foe. Rancora tried everything she could to make you turn against each other, but you persevered and stood together!

"You were strong, smart, and startacularly brave. Even what you thought was a huge misstep—accusing me of working against you—was actually beneficial, as we were able to get the real saboteur into the starlight." She glanced at Cassie, who was staring at her feet. "So no more feeling guilty, Cassie."

Cassie's glow deepened. "Star salutations, Lady Stella. That means a lot," she said earnestly.

Lady Stella continued. "The twelve of you were brought together for your strengths. Separately, you are strong and spirited, smart and talented. Together, you are an unbeatable team. Your differences could have been your undoing, but you managed to find ways to work together. And for that, I will be forever grateful."

Gemma noticed that the Star Darlings were all glowing with pride. They had grown to understand and accept each other and in the process had forged an unbreakable bond.

"Do you have any questions?" Lady Stella asked.

Vega spoke first "What about Rancora?" she said. "Who is she?"

Lady Stella frowned. "It appears that she has been plotting the downfall of Starland for quite some time, and she infiltrated Starling Academy disguised as Lady Cordial in order to gain a position of power."

"What will happen to her?" asked Gemma.

"The authorities are searching for her right now," Lady Stella explained. "She will be apprehended in due time. You can be starsure of that."

"Will we be sent back down to Wishworld again soon?" Scarlet asked hopefully.

"Eventually," the headmistress said. "At the moment, we have plenty of wish energy. There will come a time in the not-too-distant future when you will be sent back down to Wishworld. But first I'd like you all to meet with our leading wish energy scientists for a debriefing. They have a lot to learn from you and your extreme success in collecting wish energy."

Sage grinned at the news. Gemma knew she was excited to spend some time with her mother.

"One more thing," Lady Stella added. "As the twelve Star-Charmed Starlings, you may have powers that have not been discovered yet. We'll have time to study and practice and determine exactly how charmed you all are."

Leona spoke up. "You said that someday everyone will know about what we did. When do you think that will happen?"

Lady Stella nodded. "I cannot tell you exactly when, but someday all of Starland will know just how special you are."

Leona stole a sidelong glance at the other girls, a funny half smile on her face. "I guess . . ." she began slowly. "I guess it would be nice, but the truth is that the twelve of us—and you, Lady Stella—knowing it, somehow that's enough for me."

Gemma stared at Leona in disbelief. Was she serious? Didn't she want the glory and the accolades? Gemma did! But then a feeling of warmth and joy flowed through her. Actually, it *was* enough.

Lady Stella pointed into the heavens. "Not to mention that, thanks to you girls, Starland is once again twinkling brightly in the sky, beckoning Wishlings to continue to make wishes."

The girls stared down at Wishworld, a bright beacon in the dark sky. Gemma imagined that she could feel the power of all the wishes—good ones, of course—making their way to Wishworld for granting.

Gemma could hold her tongue no longer. "We're the Star Darlings—one for all and all for one!" she shouted.

Leona reached over and gave her a quick hug. "You can say that again," she said.

Gemma grinned. "We're the Star Darlings—one for all and all for one!" she repeated.

Several of the girls gasped. Tessa grabbed her arm. "Oh, no, you're taking everything literally again!" She stared deep into Gemma's auburn eyes. "Are you okay?"

But Gemma just laughed and laughed. "Too soon?" she said. "Hold your stars, big sis. I'm just kidding!"

Glossary

Afterglow: The Starling afterlife. When Starlings die, it is said that they have "begun their afterglow."

Age of Fulfillment: The age at which a Starling is considered mature enough to begin to study wish granting.

Astromuffin: A delicious baked breakfast treat.

Babsday: The second starday of the weekend. The days in order are Sweetday, Shineday, Dododay, Yumday, Lunaday, Bopday, Reliquaday, and Babsday. (Starlandians have a three-day weekend every starweek.)

Bad Wish Orbs: Orbs that are the result of bad or selfish wishes made on Wishworld. These grow dark and warped and are quickly sent to the Negative Energy Facility.

Ballum blossom sauce: A sweet sauce made from the fruit of the ballum blossom tree and used to add flavor to Starlandian food, somewhat like Wishworld ketchup.

Big Dipper Dormitory: Where third- and fourth-year students live.

Bitbat: A small winged nocturnal creature.

Bot-Bot: A Starland robot. There are Bot-Bot guards, waiters, deliverers, and guides on Starland.

Bright Day: The date a Starling is born, celebrated each year like a Wishling birthday.

Briteflowers: Small white twinkling flowers often used for decorations.

Celestial Café: Starling Academy's outstanding cafeteria.

Chatterburst: Gemma's Wish Blossom—an orange flower that turns to face whoever is near to capture attention.

Cocomoon: A sweet and creamy fruit with an iridescent glow.

Cosmic Transporter: The moving sidewalk system that transports students through dorms and across the Starling Academy campus.

Countdown Clock: A timing device on a Starling's Star-Zap. It lets them know how much time is left on a Wish Mission, which coincides with when the Wish Orb will fade.

Crystal Mountains: The most beautiful mountains on Starland. They are located across the lake from Starling Academy.

Cycle of Life: A Starling's life span. When Starlings die, they are said to have "completed their Cycle of Life."

Flash Vertical Mover: A mode of transportation similar to a Wishling elevator, only superfast.

Floozel: The Starland equivalent of a Wishworld mile.

Flutterfocus: A Starland creature similar to a Wishworld butterfly but with illuminated wings.

Galliope: A sparkly Starland creature similar to a Wishworld horse.

Garble greens: A Starland vegetable similar to spinach.

Glion: A gentle Starland creature similar in appearance to a Wishworld lion but with a multicolored glowing mane.

Glitterbees: Blue-and-orange-striped bugs that pollinate Starland flowers and produce a sweet substance called delicata.

Glorange: A glowing orange fruit. Its juice is often enjoyed at breakfast time.

Glowball: A pink fluffy flower with a sweet scent that promotes relaxation, often used in incense.

Glowfur: A small furry Starland creature with gossamer wings that eats flowers and glows.

Good Wish Orbs: Orbs that are the result of positive wishes made on Wishworld. They are planted in Wish-Houses.

Halo Hall: The building where Starling Academy classes are held.

Holo-text: A message received on a Star-Zap and projected into the air. There are also holo-albums, holo-billboards, holo-books, holo-cards, holo-communications, holo-diaries, holo-flyers, holo-letters, holo-papers, holo-pictures, and holo-place cards. Anything that would be made of paper or contain writing or images on Wishworld is a hologram on Starland.

HOS lanes: High Occupancy Starcar lanes; only vehicles with four passengers or more are allowed to use them.

Hydrong: The equivalent of a Wishworld hundred.

Illumination Library: The impressive library at Starling Academy.

Impossible Wish Orbs: Orbs that are the result of wishes made on Wishworld that are beyond the power of Starlings to grant.

Jellyjooble: A small round pink candy that is very sweet.

Kaleidoscope tree: A rare and beautiful tree whose blossoms continuously change color. When someone is said to extend the kaleidoscope tree branch, it means that they are making peace with someone else.

Keytar: A musical instrument that looks like a cross between a guitar and a keyboard.

Lightning Lounge: A place on the Starling Academy campus where students relax and socialize.

Little Dipper Dormitory: Where first- and second-year students live.

Luminous Lake: A serene and lovely lake next to the Starling Academy campus.

Mirror Mantra: A saying specific to each Star Darling that when recited gives her (and her Wisher) reassurance and strength. When a Starling recites her Mirror Mantra while looking in a mirror, she will see her true appearance reflected.

Moogle: A very short but unspecific amount of time. The word is used in expressions like "Wait just a moogle!"

Moonberries: Sweet berries that grow on Starland. They are Lady Stella's favorite snack.

Moonium: An amount similar to a Wishworld million.

Ozziefruit: Sweet plum-sized indigo fruit that grows on pink-leaved trees and is usually eaten raw or cooked in pies.

Power Crystal: The powerful stone each Star Darling receives once she has granted her first wish.

Scatterite: Gemma's Power Crystal—an orange egg-shaped stone with a smooth, sparkly surface.

Shooting stars: Speeding stars that Starlings can latch on to and ride to Wishworld.

Solar metal spike: Similar to a Wishworld nail.

Sparklehammer: Like a Wishworld hammer, but it sends out a shower of multicolored sparks whenever it strikes something.

Sparkle shower: An energy shower Starlings take every day to get clean and refresh their sparkling glow.

Star ball: An intramural sport that shares similarities with soccer on Wishworld, but star ball players use energy manipulation to control the ball.

Starcar: The primary mode of transportation for most

Starlings. These ultrasafe vehicles drive themselves on cushions of wish energy.

Star Caves: The caverns underneath Starling Academy where the Star Darlings' secret Wish-Cavern is located.

Starfl: A Starling expression of dismay.

Starkudos: An expression used to give credit to a Starling for a job well done.

Starland City: The largest city on Starland, also its capital.

Starlings: The glowing beings with sparkly skin who live on Starland.

Starmin: Sixty starsecs (or seconds) on Starland, the equivalent of a Wishworld minute.

Star Quad: The center of the Starling Academy campus. The dancing fountain, band shell, and hedge maze are located here.

Star solututions. The Starling way to say "thank you."

Star-sandwiches: Elegant star-shaped sandwiches with various tasty fillings.

Starshine: An endearment used by loved ones, similar to "sunshine" or "darling."

Starshine Day: A special holiday when students get the day off from school and celebrate with food, music, games, science and art fairs, light shows, parades, sporting events, and more.

Staryear: A time period on Starland, the equivalent of a Wishworld year.

Star-Zap: The ultimate smartphone that Starlings use for all communications. It has myriad features.

Supernova: A stellar explosion. Also used colloquially, meaning "really angry," as in "She went supernova when she found out the bad news."

Time of Letting Go: One of the four seasons on Starland. It falls between the warmest season and the coldest, similar to fall on Wishworld.

Time of Lumiere: The warmest season on Starland, similar to summer on Wishworld.

Time of New Beginnings: Similar to spring on Wishworld, this is the season that follows the coldest time of year; it's when plants and trees come into bloom.

Time of Shadows: The coldest season of the year on Starland, similar to winter on Wishworld.

Toothlight: A high-tech gadget Starlings use to clean their teeth.

Twinkelopes: Majestic herd animals. Males have imposing antlers with star-shaped horns, and females have iridescent manes and flowing tails.

Wish Blossom: The bloom that appears from a Wish Orb after its wish is granted.

Wish energy: The positive energy that is released when a wish is granted. Wish energy powers everything on Starland.

Wisher: The Wishling who has made the wish that is being granted.

Wish-Granters: Starlings whose job is to travel down to Wishworld to help make wishes come true and collect wish energy.

Wish-House: The place where Wish Orbs are planted and cared for until they sparkle. Once the orb's wish is granted, it becomes a Wish Blossom.

Wishlings: The inhabitants of Wishworld.

Wish Mission: The task a Starling undertakes when she travels to Wishworld to help grant a wish.

Wish Orb: The form a wish takes on Wishworld before traveling to Starland. There it will grow and sparkle when it's time to grant the wish.

Wish Pendant: A gadget that absorbs and transports wish energy, helps Starlings locate their Wishers, and changes a Starling's appearance. Each Wish Pendant holds a different special power for its Star Darling.

Wishworld: The planet Starland relies on for wish energy. The beings on Wishworld know it by another name—Earth.

Wishworld Outfit Selector: A program on each Star-Zap that accesses Wishworld fashions for Starlings to wear to blend in on their Wish Missions.

Wishworld Surveillance Deck: A platform located high above the campus, where Starling Academy students go to observe Wishlings through high-powered telescopes.

Zing: A traditional Starling breakfast drink. It can be enjoyed hot or iced.

Acknowledgments

It is impossible to list all of our gratitude, but we will try.

Our most precious gift and greatest teacher, Halo; we love you more than there are stars in the sky . . . punashaku. To the rest of our crazy, awesome, unique tribe—thank you for teaching us to go for our dreams. Integrity. Strength. Love. Foundation. Family. Grateful. Mimi Muldoon—from your star doodling to naming our Star Darlings, your artistry, unconditional love, and inspiration is infinite. Didi Muldoon—your belief and support in us is only matched by your fierce protection and massive-hearted guidance. Gail. Queen G. Your business sense and witchy wisdom are legendary. Frank—you are missed and we know you are watching over us all. Along with Tutu, Nana, and Deda, who are always present, gently guiding us in spirit. To our colorful, totally genius, and bananas siblings Patrick, Moon, Diva, and Dweezil—there is more creativity and humor in those four names than most people experience in a lifetime. Blessed. To our magical nieces—Mathilda, Zola, Ceylon, and Mia—the Star Darlings adore you and so do we. Our witchy cuzzie fairy godmothers—Ane and Gina. Our fairy fashion godfather, Paris. Our sweet Panay. Teeta and Freddy—we love you all so much. And our four-legged fur babies—Sandwich, Luna, Figgy, and Pinky Star.

The incredible Barry Waldo, our SD partner. Sent to us from above in perfect timing. Your expertise and friendship are beyond words. We love you and Gary to the moon and back. Long live the manifestation room!

Catherine Daly—the stars shined brightly upon us the day we aligned with you. Your talent and inspiration are otherworldly; our appreciation cannot be expressed in words. Many heartfelt hugs for you and the adorable Oonagh.

To our beloved Disney family. Thank you for believing in us. Wendy Lefkon, our master guide and friend through this entire journey. Stephanie Lurie, for being the first to believe in Star Darlings. Suzanne Murphy, who helped every step of the way. Jeanne Mosure, we fell in love with you the first time we met, and Star Darlings wouldn't be what it is without you. Andrew Sugerman, thank you so much for all your support.

Our team . . . Devon (pony pants) and our Monsterfoot crew—so grateful. Richard Scheltinga—our angel and protector. Chris Abramson—thank you! Special appreciation to Richard Thompson, John LaViolette, Swanna, Mario, and Sam.

To our friends old and new—we are so grateful to be on this rad journey that is life with you all. Fay. Jorja. Chandra. Sananda. Sandy. Kathryn. Louise. What wisdom and strength you share. Ruth, Mike, and the rest of our magical Wagon Wheel bunch—how lucky we are. How inspiring you are. We love you.

Last—we have immeasurable gratitude for every person we've met along our journey, for all the good and the bad; it is all a gift. From the bottom of our hearts we thank you for touching our lives.

Shana Muldoon Zappa is a jewelry designer and writer who was born and raised in Los Angeles. She has an endless imagination and a passion to inspire positivity through her many artistic endeavors. She and her husband, Ahmet Zappa, collaborated on Star Darlings especially for their magical little girl and biggest inspiration, Halo Violetta Zappa.

Ahmet Zappa is the *New York Times* best-selling author of *Because I'm Your Dad* and *The Monstrous Memoirs of a Mighty McFearless.* He writes and produces films and television shows and loves pancakes, unicorns, and making funny faces for Halo and Shana.

Check out an excerpt from
the next Star Darlings book,
Good Wish Gone Bad

Starling Academy was positively glowing. The buildings, the fountains, the trees, and even the moving Cosmic Transporter sidewalks looked more dazzling than they had in recent memory. Off in the distance, the Crystal Mountains also appeared to stand a bit taller, prouder, and brighter as the reflection of their multicolored peaks bounced off the shimmering azure surface of the Luminous Lake below. All signs of the negative wish energy that had been plaguing everything from the fruit orchards to the Starling Academy students themselves had faded away, almost as though it had been nothing more than a bad dream—and it was entirely thanks to the twelve star-charmed Star Darlings!

"Have you ever seen the campus look more beautiful?" marveled Sage. Her long, lavender braids were also shinier than they had been in quite some time, and they bounced behind her as she and the other Star Darlings hurried past classmates who were heading to the Celestial Café for dinner.

Instead of going to their own evening meal, however, the girls were on their way to Lady Stella's office. The head-mistress had summoned them on their Star-Zaps, instructing them to join her right away for an important meeting. In spite of the urgent tone of the holo-text, Sage felt certain that Lady Stella simply wanted to congratulate the Star Darlings on the successful completion of their top-secret wish missions. Together, they had collected enough positive wish energy to help ensure that everything on Starland would be powered for countless staryears to come.

"I've never seen the *world* look more beautiful," said Sage's roommate, Cassie, her eyes widening with delight behind her star-shaped glasses as the girls continued along the Cosmic Transporter.

"It *is* super celestial—but how long do you think this meeting is going to last?" Tessa wondered. "I'm hungry!" Just like her gourmet chef mother, the emerald-haired third-year student was almost always thinking about food.

"Do you think she's got more wish missions for us?" asked Libby. It had been a long while since she'd gone on her journey down to Wishworld and, as exciting as it was to know that all twelve Star Darlings had completed their missions, she couldn't wait to go on another one.

"I doubt it. We've already done all we can," scoffed Scarlet, shoving her hands into the front pocket of her sparkling red hoodie and rolling her eyes as the girls made their way into Halo Hall.

A few moments later, they arrived at the door to Lady Stella's office, which was cracked open in anticipation of their visit.

"Girls!" The elegant headmistress stood up from her desk, breathing a sigh of relief as she smoothed down the fabric of her sparkly silver gown. "I thought you'd never get here. Come, let's go down to the Wish-Cavern at once."

"I knew it!" Libby tossed her long, bubblegum-pink hair proudly and shot a triumphant smile in Scarlet's direction as Lady Stella opened the hidden door in her office wall. Why else would they be going to the Wish-Cavern unless she had more missions for them?

The girls followed their headmistress down the secret staircase to the dark caves beneath the school, shivering as they made their way through the chilly air, past the dripping rock formations and toward the door to their own secret Wish-House. It was a special room that had been built exclusively for the Star Darlings and their uniquely powerful wish missions.

But unlike the times they'd been in the Wish-House before, this time, at the foot of a large golden waterfall in the gleaming light-soaked room, a round table had been set up with all sorts of treats—including an enormous zoomberry cake and fancy crystal glasses full of sparkling puckerup juice at each place setting. Above the table, a giant holo-banner floated in mid-air, emblazoned with large, glittery gold letters that spelled out the words CONGRATULATIONS, STAR DARLINGS!

"Well, girls, this is quite a momentous day, indeed," Lady Stella began as they all settled into their chairs, which immediately adjusted to their respective heights and weights for optimum comfort. The headmistress raised her long, delicate glass. "I cannot begin to tell you how pleased I am with what you've each accomplished. Thanks to your hard work and diligence in completing your wish missions, there is now more positive wish energy on Starland than ever before!"

The girls all exchanged excited glances, beaming with pride as they too raised their glasses and each took a sip. "Star salutations, Lady Stella!" they replied in almost perfect unison.

"And to you," Lady Stella said softly as she cut into the cake, serving each girl a generous slice and encouraging them to eat—which they were more than happy to do. After all, it was highly unusual for young Starlings to be permitted to have dessert before dinner!

As the girls happily chatted, reminiscing about some of the best parts of their missions, Lady Stella glanced around the table at each one of them with a faraway look in her eyes.

"Why aren't you eating?" Tessa asked the headmistress between bites.

Lady Stella pressed her bright red lips together before attempting a smile. But it was no use. She couldn't pretend with them. "Star Darlings . . ." she said, inhaling deeply and closing her eyes for a moment, "we do have much to celebrate—but I suppose I should also tell you that even greater challenges may lie ahead for us all."

The celebratory mood in the air suddenly became thick with nervous energy. What was the headmistress referring to, exactly?

"As you know, everyone at Starling Academy was completely deceived by Lady Cordial, who was our Director of Admissions. She was someone I trusted and valued as one of my closest confidantes." Lady Stella sighed and shook her head as she stared down at the table. "I genuinely believed that she was our friend—but, in fact, she was not Lady Cordial at all. She was Rancora in disguise."

As soon as Lady Stella mentioned that dreaded name, the golden light in the Wish-Cavern flickered and dimmed ever so slightly, and the Star Darlings all felt an icy chill run down their spines. They frowned and nodded solemnly. Although they had managed to avoid discussing Lady Cordial for the past week, they of course knew that at some point her name—and the far more terrifying name of Rancora—would come up again. They had simply hoped it wouldn't be quite so soon.

"But she's gone now," Gemma pointed out, her wavy orange ponytail glimmering.

"Well, yes, she has left Starling Academy—that's true," Lady Stella acknowledged. "However, we don't know *where* she's gone or what she might be planning to do next. So, although I'm hopeful that she'll keep her distance and stay far, far away from the school grounds, I believe that she may be planning something bigger—something that will place Starland in even greater danger."

"Wh-what could be more dangerous than the negative energy she was releasing?" asked Cassie, who began trembling so much that she had to set down her fork.

"Yeah—and how much more can she really do?" Vega wondered. "You said that there's more positive wish energy on Starland than ever before—plus, we already defeated her, when we united our twelve power crystals. Won't that be enough to stop Rancora again, even if she tries to do something else?"

"That is my hope—but I'm still trying to find the missing page that I believe Rancora, or, rather, Lady Cordial, stole from the oracle," Lady Stella replied, referring to the ancient text that foretold of the twelve girls and the role they would play in saving Starland in the first place. "While I spend the next few days continuing my search, I suggest that you all put this out of your minds and get some rest. You've been through so much and will be needing your energy—not only for your studies, but in the event that I require your assistance again. Of course, that will depend on what I'm able to find out."

While the girls quietly pondered everything Lady Stella had said, she tried to encourage them to continue their celebration, offering them more cake and juice. But Tessa was the only one who still had any sort of an appetite left.

"I'm sorry, girls," Lady Stella said with a frown. "I hadn't intended to bring this up with you today—but it's important for you to be aware of the potential challenges that may lie ahead. Try not to worry too much. I *will* come up with a solution."

"We know you will," said Libby, her bright pink eyes gleaming with positive energy. "And we can help as soon as you need us!"

"Yes!" agreed Clover, lightly tapping the rim of her purple fedora. "We'll do whatever it takes. Right, Star Darlings?"

"Right!" the girls all cheered.

But as they got up from their comfy chairs and shuffled out of the Wish-House, the mood was anything but cheery.

The next morning, every last one of the Star Darlings woke up early. In fact, most of them had hardly slept at all. Vega had been especially restless, plagued by nightmares about Rancora, with her piercing purple eyes and ashen skin and hair, the blazing pink collar of her long, tattered gray gown rising behind her head like the fiery flames of doom. Sitting up in bed, Vega leaned back against her headboard and began to record holo-notes on her Star-Zap about everything she had observed about Lady Cordial. She still couldn't believe that the frumpy-dumpy director of admissions had been the evil Rancora in disguise all that time!

"You couldn't sleep, either?" Piper asked in a soft ethereal voice from her side of the room as she pushed off her cozy aqua comforter and pulled her long seafoam-green hair up into a high ponytail.

"No." Vega rubbed her blue eyes and shook her head. Her chin-length cobalt bob looked perfect as ever, in spite of the fact that she was still in bed. "I can't stop thinking about

Lady Cordial—or, you know, *Rancora*. I should have realized that she might still be plotting something terrible."

"I know." Piper slid on her fluffy slippers, closed her eyes, and took several deep, cleansing breaths. "I've been having visions ever since Lady Stella mentioned her name yesterday."

Vega wrinkled her nose. Sometimes Piper's visions could be kind of out there—but other times they had proven to be right on target. "What kind of visions?"

"Well . . ." Piper took a few more deep breaths. "It's kind of scary."

"Tell me!" Vega demanded.

"All right. I saw Rancora in a big dark cloud—but she kept changing into Lady Cordial and then back into herself," Piper recounted. "Every time she changed into Rancora, she tried to pull us into the cloud, too, and she kept saying she wanted us to join forces with her."

"Us—who is *us*?" Vega's eyes darkened with worry.

"All twelve of us—the Star Darlings," Piper said.

"Oh, my stars!" Vega jumped out of bed and began pacing around the room. "What if you're right? What if she tries to turn us into her negative energy minions? Her toxic trainees! We need to figure out exactly what Rancora is planning and find a way to stop her—like, *now*."

Piper widened her eyes, mystified by Vega's words. "But Lady Stella said she was going to search for the missing page from the oracle and *then* figure out what needs to be done. She told us we needed to wait to hear from her. She said we needed to rest up so we could get our energy back."

"I know," Vega said tersely. "But I don't want to sit around waiting—or resting—when we could be helping. We don't want to be caught off guard, right? The more prepared we are the better!"

Piper shrugged and sat back in bed while Vega raced around her side of the room, grabbing her toothlight and rushing out to take a sparkle shower. Within minutes, she was back and getting dressed in a shiny blue blazer over a matching tunic, with sparkly tights and ankle boots.

"What are you going to do?" Piper asked.

"We need to go to the Illumination Library!" Vega informed her.

"The library? Why?" Piper looked blankly at her roommate.

"So we can try to figure out exactly where Rancora came from," Vega explained. "There's *got* to be a holo-book there that will point us in the right direction! Hurry up and get ready. I'll holo-text everyone to meet us there!"

"Okay," Piper agreed reluctantly.

A few of the Star Darlings were already out in front of the Illumination Library when Vega and Piper showed up, some looking more awake than others.

"What's this all about?" asked Adora, who was flawlessly styled, as usual, in shimmering indigo leggings with knee-high boots and a chic fitted dress, her pale blue hair piled high in a fashionably messy updo.

"Yeah, what's happening?" echoed Adora's roommate, Tessa, stifling a yawn as she popped the last bite of a glorange-spice muffin into her mouth.

"I'll tell you when the others get here," Vega replied, tapping her foot as she stared impatiently across the Star Quad. Finally, she could see the rest of the girls moving toward the library on the Cosmic Transporter.

"What's up?" Libby asked when she arrived. "We got here as fast as we could!"

"Piper and I were up all night, thinking about the whole Lady Cordial—or Rancora—situation," Vega explained as the others all gathered round. "Piper had a vision that Lady Cordial kept turning into Rancora and was trying to pull us into some sort of dark cloud, insisting she wanted us to join forces with her or something."

"Seriously?" Scarlet crossed her arms in frustration. "You called us all the way here to tell us *that*?"

"No." Vega glared at Scarlet, whose short fuchsia hair was slightly messy from sleep. "I called you here because obviously there's a lot more to Rancora than any of us realize, and we need to know more about her if we're going to figure out what she might be planning to do to us—or to Starland—next. Lady Stella may be doing her own research, but I think we should start doing a bit of our own, too!"

"What kind of research?" asked Libby, always eager to help in any way she could.

"Well, for starters, we should see what we can find out about Lady Cordial, since that's who Rancora was in disguise," Vega proposed.

"That's not a bad idea," Sage noted. "There's got to be some information about her in the faculty pages of the school staryearbooks."

"Exactly!" Vega agreed.

"I don't see how that's going to help," Scarlet protested. "What are the staryearbooks going to tell us that we—and especially Lady Stella—don't already know?"

"I say we give it a try," Leona chimed in, giving her shiny golden curls a confident pat. "If we *do* find out something useful, Lady Stella will think we're even bigger stars than we already are."

"I agree," said Sage.

"Me too." Tessa nodded.

"Ugh. Fine." Scarlet rolled her eyes, giving in only after all the others had voiced their support.

"Excellent," Vega said with a smile, leading the way into the library.

With most of the Starling Academy campus still asleep, it was even quieter inside than usual. The twelve girls made their way through the vast stacks of holo-books and up the winding staircase to the section where the staryearbooks were located. The tomes contained holo-images of every student and faculty member who had ever been at Starling Academy, along with detailed records of everything that had happened during each school staryear since the very first class had enrolled.

"So what are we looking for, exactly?" asked Gemma, accessing the holo-pages of a recent staryearbook as she sat down on a plush orange couch and began scanning through them. "This says Lady Cordial has been at Starling Academy for two years and she's helped to make the school what it is today."

"Ha—only because nothing's been written about *us* yet!" Leona grinned proudly while Vega sat down next to Gemma and tapped on the image of Lady Cordial, eager to see if anything more useful might pop up.

Alas, all she saw was the director of admissions shuffling from her office to Lady Stella's office, then back to her office, with an occasional moment where she spilled something or tripped. *That* was helping to make the school what it was today?

"There has to be more information about her than this," Vega said with a frown, taking the book from Gemma and scrolling through it some more.

"I'm kind of with Scarlet—even if we found more information about Lady Cordial, what would it really tell us?" asked Adora, sitting down next to Vega. "Isn't *Rancora* the one we need to investigate?"

"Yes, but they're one and the same," Vega pointed out as she continued to scroll through the pages, moving farther and farther back in time.

"True, but we might find something more informative— something she was hiding—if we go to her office, or maybe even her old residence in Prof Row," Adora pointed out.

"Adora's probably right," Sage agreed.

"She's *totally* right!" Scarlet said.

"Oh, my stars!" Piper suddenly called out. She had wandered off and found a much older staryearbook, which she was now gazing at in wide-eyed wonder.

"What?" Vega asked, leaping up from the couch and racing over to grab the holo-book from her roommate before returning to the couch with it.

"What is it, Vega?" Sage asked, positioning herself behind Vega so she could get a better view.

"It's . . . it's . . . Lady Stella!" Vega gasped as she glanced over at Piper. "Right?"

"Uh-huh." Piper nodded.

"So?" Scarlet huffed.

"No—I mean, it's Lady Stella when she was *our* age," Vega elaborated. "When she was just . . . *student* Stella."

That was enough to distract everyone from the task at hand, at least for the moment.

"Oooh! I want to see!" Gemma grabbed the book from Vega and studied the holo-page intently.

Even Scarlet leaned in a little closer to see the photo of two teenage girls with their hands clasped. The tall sophisticated one with long golden-pink hair and a Bright Day crown on her head was most certainly a younger version of their headmistress.

"Holy stars," exclaimed Adora, reaching over to grab the book from Gemma. "Look how super celestial that dress is! And those boots! She was so beautiful, even back then."

"She and her friend look so happy," Gemma noticed.

"C'mon, guys," Scarlet said. "Looking at old holo-photos of Lady Stella won't help us figure out anything about Lady Cordial or Rancora or whatever you want to call her."

"I'm actually getting a strange feeling this staryearbook is really important," murmured Piper.

"Piper thinks this is important. Let's take a quick look," Adora urged. "Then we can go check out Lady Cordial's office. It's not like we have to be in class for a while, anyway."

"Actually, I think we should do more than take a quick look," Vega said. "As long as we're going into this old staryearbook, I might as well holo-hack into it. That way, it'll automatically link us to any important info from any other relevant holo-document, like a journal or letter."

"Wow, that's so cool, Vega," said Cassie, impressed with Vega's tech skills.

So, as the girls all gathered around, Vega tapped on the image of young Stella, and a holographic video detailing her time at Starling Academy—long before she became headmistress—began to play before their eyes. . . .